THE
Harry Potter
WIZARDING ALMANAC

SCHOLASTIC INC.

Library of Congress Cataloging-in-Publication Data available
ISBN 978-1-339-01814-0

10 9 8 7 6 5 4 3 2 1   23 24 25 26 27

MIX
Paper | Supporting responsible forestry
FSC® C144853
FSC
www.fsc.org

Printed in China
First edition, October 2023

THE OFFICIAL
MAGICAL COMPANION TO

J.K. ROWLING'S

HARRY POTTER BOOKS

THE
Harry Potter
WIZARDING
ALMANAC

ILLUSTRATED BY

∘ PETER GOES ∘ LOUISE LOCKHART ∘
∘ WEITONG MAI ∘ OLIA MUZA ∘
∘ PHAM QUANG PHUC ∘ LEVI PINFOLD ∘
∘ TOMISLAV TOMIĆ ∘

PETER GOES

LOUISE LOCKHART

WEITONG MAI

OLIA MUZA

PHAM QUANG PHUC

LEVI PINFOLD

TOMISLAV TOMIĆ

LOUISE LOCKHART

Louise Lockhart studied illustration at the Glasgow School of Art and is now an independent illustrator and printmaker based in the UK. Louise's style is influenced by her love for vintage print ephemera and bright, bold colors. Take a moment to sample her mouth-watering sweets and treats on the Hogwarts Express trolley; then enjoy her brilliant broomsticks and magnificent Yule Ball robes.

PHAM QUANG PHUC

Pham Quang Phuc is a children's book illustrator from Vietnam with a rich and decorative style. He has illustrated many books, and considers storytelling a way to balance his life. Among other prizes, Quang Phuc is a winner of The ASEAN Children's Book Illustrator Best in Fiction award. Look out for his truly magnificent magical maps, noble Quidditch champions, and sky-swooping, fire-blazing dragons.

PETER GOES

Peter Goes is a freelance artist and picture book illustrator living in Belgium. He has also worked as a stage manager and studied animation at the Royal Academy of Fine Arts (KASK) in Ghent. Peter combines playful witches, wizards, and magical creatures with an incredibly rich level of intricacy. Pore over his spectacular vision of Gringotts Wizarding Bank, the hushed wonder of the Marauder's Map, and the shelves of the Hogwarts library.

OLIA MUZA

Olia Muza was born in Uman, Ukraine. After studying graphic design, she discovered her passion for book illustration and hasn't looked back since. Olia is a remarkable storyteller who creates fun, magic, and even mayhem with her work. She invites you to explore the head-spinning ways through the wizarding world, enjoy out-of-control mischief at Weasleys' Wizard Wheezes, and share the spirit of Christmas at Hogwarts.

TOMISLAV TOMIĆ

Tomislav Tomić lives with his family in Croatia. He graduated from the Academy of Fine Art in Zagreb. He has always loved making picture books and already had work published when he was in high school. Tomislav creates exquisite and intensely detailed pen-and-ink drawings, allowing readers to look inside a host of magical places. Visit his incredible views of the Burrow; number twelve, Grimmauld Place; and Dumbledore's office.

WEITONG MAI

Weitong Mai is a Chinese-Canadian artist now based in London. She has won many awards and is a visiting lecturer at the University of Creative Arts. Weitong uses a soft, rich, and unusual palette to evoke simmering potion fumes and shimmering streams of wand magic. Seek out her apothecary shelves, sleeping Mandrakes, and her enchanting collection of magical objects small enough to fit into a wizard's pocket.

LEVI PINFOLD

Levi Pinfold has been drawing from his imagination for as long as he can remember. He has published many acclaimed books, and is a winner of the prestigious CILIP Kate Greenaway Medal. Born in the Forest of Dean, he now lives in northern New South Wales, Australia. Seek out Levi's Knight Bus as it bumps along through the London fog, explore the House common rooms, and peer into the thorns and thickets of his Forbidden Forest.

CONTENTS

1 THE WITCHES AND WIZARDS WHO LIVED

2 SPORTS, PEOPLE, AND EVERYTHING WIZARDING

(or S.P.E.W. for short)

3 SPELLBINDING SPACES AND PECULIAR PLACES

ALBUS DUMBLEDORE

4 AN INVITATION TO HOGWARTS

5 SPELLS, CHARMS, AND UNFORGIVABLE CURSES

6 MINISTERING MAGIC AND INSPIRING INSTITUTIONS

7 BEASTS, BEINGS, AND BOTANICALS

A WIZARDING TIMELINE

The first game of Quidditch in its earliest form

The earliest known gathering of the Wizengamot, the Wizard High Court

EARLY 1500s The Leaky Cauldron is built at number one, Diagon Alley

1000s

1400s

The Order of Merlin is first awarded

900s The founding of Hogwarts School of Witchcraft and Wizardry

DRACO DORMIENS NUNQUAM TITILLANDUS

by Godric Gryffindor, Rowena Ravenclaw, Helga Hufflepuff, and Salazar Slytherin

1544

LATE 1500s TO EARLY 1600s St. Mungo's Hospital for Magical Maladies and Injuries is established

O.M.

900s–1000s Hengist of Woodcroft founds Hogsmeade village

900s–1000s Hogwarts' founders create the Sorting Hat

900s–1000s Salazar Slytherin departs from Hogwarts after an argument about who should be accepted into the school

382 BC The Ollivander family starts making wands

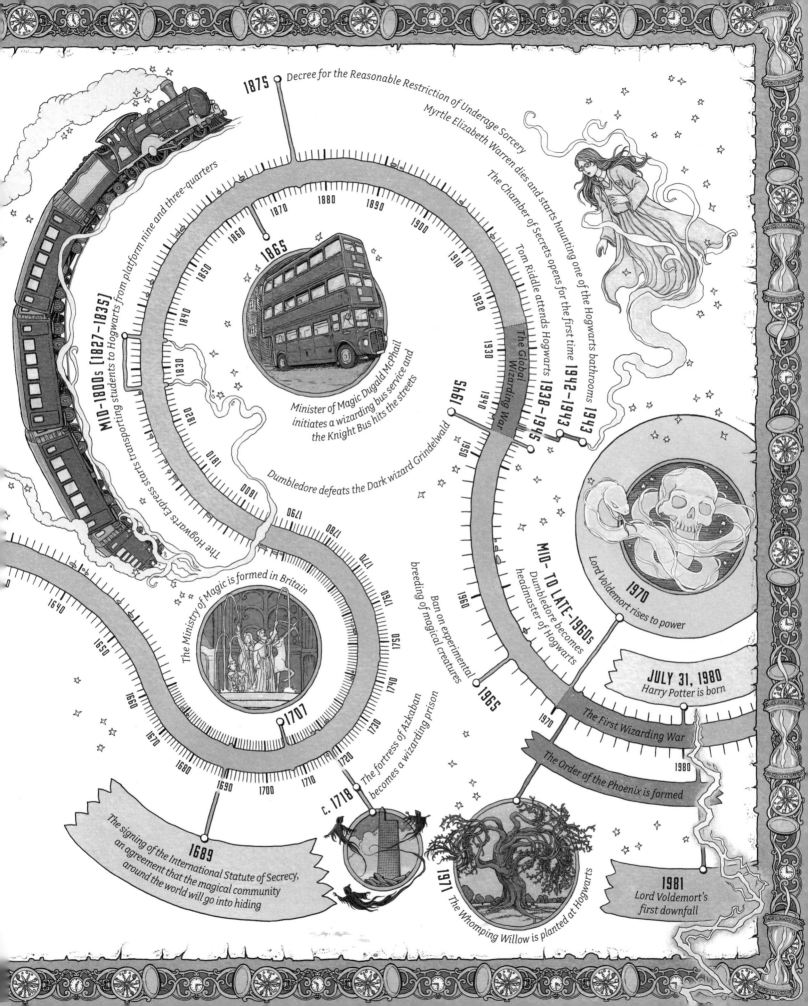

1875 — Decree for the Reasonable Restriction of Underage Sorcery

Myrtle Elizabeth Warren dies and starts haunting one of the Hogwarts bathrooms

The Chamber of Secrets opens for the first time 1942–1943

Tom Riddle attends Hogwarts 1938–1945

MID-1800s (1827–1835)
The Hogwarts Express starts transporting students to Hogwarts from platform nine and three-quarters

1865
Minister of Magic Dugald McPhail initiates a wizarding bus service and the Knight Bus hits the streets

The Global Wizarding War

Dumbledore defeats the Dark wizard Grindelwald 1945

The Ministry of Magic is formed in Britain

1707

Ban on experimental breeding of magical creatures

MID- TO LATE-1960s
Dumbledore becomes headmaster of Hogwarts

1970
Lord Voldemort rises to power

JULY 31, 1980
Harry Potter is born

The First Wizarding War

The fortress of Azkaban becomes a wizarding prison
c. 1718

1965

The Order of the Phoenix is formed

1689
The signing of the International Statute of Secrecy, an agreement that the magical community around the world will go into hiding

1971 The Whomping Willow is planted at Hogwarts

1981
Lord Voldemort's first downfall

Harry discovers he's a wizard **JULY 31, 1991**

Vault 713 in Gringotts Bank is broken into but nothing is stolen

1991 MAY
1991 JUNE
1991 JULY
1991 AUGUST
1991 SEPTEMBER
1991 OCTOBER
1991 NOVEMBER
1991 DECEMBER

1991 APRIL
1991 MARCH
1991 FEBRUARY
1991 JANUARY

SEPTEMBER 1, 1991

Cornelius Fudge becomes Minister of Magic

1990

Harry Potter arrives at Hogwarts

1989
1988
1987
1986
1985
1984
1983
1982
1981

Harry arrives at Privet Drive

1981

> " 'What we need,' said Dumbledore slowly, and his light blue eyes moved from Harry to Hermione, 'is more *time*.' "

1992

Lord Voldemort resurfaces in the wizarding world

1992

1992 The Chamber of Secrets opens for the second time

DAILY PROPHET
EDITOR BARNABAS CUFFE
BLACK STILL AT LARGE

Sirius Black breaks out of Azkaban

1993

1993

"'What's comin' will come, an' we'll meet it when it does.'"
RUBEUS HAGRID

The Battle of Hogwarts 1998

1998

Pius Thicknesse becomes Minister of Magic 1997–1998

JULY 31, 1997
Harry's seventeenth birthday

1997

Lord Voldemort rises again 1995

1995

1995

Albus Dumbledore recalls the Order of the Phoenix

Dolores Umbridge becomes Hogwarts High Inquisitor

1996 Rufus Scrimgeour becomes Minister of Magic

The Second Wizarding War

1995

1994

The Triwizard Tournament is held at Hogwarts

The 422nd Quidditch World Cup takes place

1994

1994

1996

1996
Mass breakout of prisoners from Azkaban

1

THE WITCHES AND WIZARDS WHO LIVED

Many characters have a part to play in Harry Potter's destiny. Explore the unique journey of the Boy Who Lived through his unforgettable first encounters, loyal protectors, and lifelong bonds. Meet Ron Weasley, Hermione Granger, and other allies, and come face-to-face with He-Who-Must-Not-Be-Named. Discover the links that bind wizarding families and friendships both lost and found, and remember that there are more important things than books and cleverness.

HOME

Number four, Privet Drive,
Little Whinging, Surrey

EYE COLOR

Green

"'Everyone thinks I'm special . . .
but I don't know anything about
magic at all. How can they expect
great things? I'm famous and I can't
even remember what I'm famous for.'"

"Expelliarmus!"

WAND

Phoenix tail
feather, holly,
11 inches

"'Harry — yer a wizard.'
RUBEUS HAGRID"

Nimbus Two Thousand

SPECIAL SKILLS

- Hogwarts's youngest
  Quidditch Seeker in a
  century (Gryffindor)
- Speaks Parseltongue
- Defense Against the
  Dark Arts

PATRONUS

Stag

HARRY'S ACCIDENTAL MAGIC

- Growing his hair overnight
- Jumping onto the roof at his
  Muggle school
- Turning his teacher's wig blue
- Shrinking his ugly jumper
- Vanishing the glass of a
  snake tank
- Shattering a wineglass
- Inflating Marjorie Dursley
- Priori Incantatem, the reverse
  spell effect

Firebolt

BOGGART

Dementor

HEDWIG

Mr. H. Potter
The Cupboard under the Stairs
4 Privet Drive
Little Whinging
Surrey

HARRY JAMES POTTER

DATE OF BIRTH July 31, 1980 **HOGWARTS HOUSE** Gryffindor

'Trouble usually finds me.'

'I don't go looking for trouble. . . .

'You shall not harm Harry Potter!'

DOBBY THE HOUSE-ELF

Marauder's Map

ALSO KNOWN AS

The Boy Who Lived
The Chosen One
Undesirable No. 1
Potty (*Draco Malfoy
and Peeves*)

⚡ 17

Invisibility Cloak

FAMILY

James Potter (father, wizard), **Lily Potter** (mother, witch),
Sirius Black (godfather, wizard), **Petunia Dursley** (aunt, Muggle),
Vernon Dursley (uncle, Muggle), **Dudley Dursley** (cousin, Muggle)

The Letters from No One

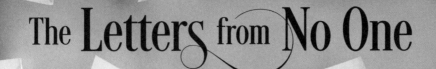

Mr. H. Potter
The Floor
Hut-on-the-Rock
The Sea

Mr. H. Potter
Room 17
Railview Hotel
Cokeworth

HOGWARTS SCHOOL
of WITCHCRAFT and WIZARDRY

HEADMASTER: ALBUS DUMBLEDORE

(Order of Merlin, First Class, Grand Sorc., Chf. Warlock,
Supreme Mugwump, International Confed. of Wizards)

Dear Mr. Potter,

We are pleased to inform you that you have been accepted
at Hogwarts School of Witchcraft and Wizardry. Please
find enclosed a list of all necessary books and equipment.
Term begins on September 1. We await your owl by no
later than July 31.

Yours sincerely,

Minerva McGonagall

Deputy Headmistress

Dear Professor Dumbledore,
Given Harry his letter.
Taking him to buy his things tomorrow.
Weather's horrible. Hope you're well.

Hagrid

Mr. H. Potter
The Smallest Bedroom
4 Privet Drive
Little Whinging
Surrey

Packing for Hogwarts

HOGWARTS EXPRESS
SEPTEMBER 1ST 11 O'CLOCK · KING'S CROSS STATION
PLATFORM **9¾**

"**H**arry took the parchment envelope out of his pocket. 'Good,' said Hagrid. 'There's a list there of everything yeh need.'"

FIRST-YEAR STUDENTS WILL REQUIRE:

Three sets of plain work robes (black)

One plain pointed hat (black) for day wear

One set of brass scales

One telescope

Students may also bring an owl **OR** a cat **OR** a toad

One wand

One cauldron (pewter, standard size two)

PLEASE NOTE that all pupils' clothes should carry name tags

One set of glass or crystal phials

One pair of protective gloves (dragon hide or similar)

One winter cloak (black, silver fastenings)

PARENTS ARE REMINDED THAT FIRST YEARS ARE **NOT ALLOWED** THEIR OWN BROOMSTICKS

COURSE BOOKS

All students should have a copy of each of the following:

The Standard Book of Spells (Grade 1) by Miranda Goshawk

A History of Magic by Bathilda Bagshot

Magical Theory by Adalbert Waffling

A Beginners' Guide to Transfiguration by Emeric Switch

One Thousand Magical Herbs and Fungi by Phyllida Spore

Magical Draughts and Potions by Arsenius Jigger

Fantastic Beasts and Where to Find Them by Newt Scamander

The Dark Forces: A Guide to Self-Protection by Quentin Trimble

HARRY POTTER

19

Find everything you need in Diagon Alley on page 72 ➜

FAMILY, FRIENDS, and LIFELONG BONDS

The Cupboard under the Stairs

Beginnings

20

NEW FRIENDS AND ALLIES

Cedric Diggory

Nymphadora Tonks

Severus Snape

Charlie Weasley

Remus Lupin

George Weasley

Minerva McGonagall

Neville Longbottom

WATCHING OVER HIM

FIRST ENCOUNTERS

WELCOME TO THE WIZARDING WORLD

Luna Lovegood

Albus Dumbledore

Petunia Dursley

Hermione Granger

Sirius Black

Cho Chang

Ron Weasley

Rubeus Hagrid

Vernon Dursley

James Potter

HARRY

Fleur
Delacour

Molly
Weasley

Bill
Weasley

HOGWARTS
TEACHERS

Fred
Weasley

Filius
Flitwick

Kingsley
Shacklebolt

Hedwig

Percy
Weasley

Arthur
Weasley

Pomona
Sprout

Dudley
Dursley

Ginny
Weasley

GODRIC'S
HOLLOW

PRIVET
DRIVE

Garrick
Ollivander

Sybill
Trelawney

Draco
Malfoy

Dobby

Alastor "Mad-Eye"
Moody

POTTER

Lily
Potter

Hogwarts

RONALD BILIUS WEASLEY

DATE OF BIRTH March 1, 1980   **HOGWARTS HOUSE** Gryffindor

"'*Don't let the Muggles get you down!*'"

Ron's second wand (unicorn hair, willow, 14 inches)

BOGGART
Spiders

PIGWIDGEON

QUIDDITCH TEAM
Chudley Cannons

ALSO KNOWN AS

Ron *(friends)*
Ronald *(teachers, authority figures, Auntie Muriel, George, Luna Lovegood, Zacharias Smith)*
Ickle Ronniekins *(Fred and George)*
Ronnie *(Molly, Fred, and George)*
Wheezy *(Dobby)*
Won-Won *(Lavender Brown)*
Roonil Wazlib *(a faulty Spell-Checking Quill)*
You — complete — *arse* — Ronald — Weasley! *(Hermione Granger)*

HOME
The Burrow

HAND-ME-DOWNS

- Percy's rat, Scabbers
- Charlie's wand
- Bill's school robes
- Charlie's cauldron
- Charlie's broomstick

"'And from now on, I don't care if my tea-leaves spell *die, Ron, die* — I'm just chucking them in the bin where they belong.'"

22

PARENTS

Arthur Weasley (father, wizard, works for the Misuse of Muggle Artifacts Office), **Molly Weasley** (mother, witch)

SIBLINGS

Bill (curse-breaker for Gringotts Bank), **Charlie** (studies dragons in Romania), **Percy**, **Fred**, **George**, **Ginny**

WAND Initially used Charlie's old wand (unicorn hair, ash, 12 inches)

PATRONUS
Jack Russell terrier

SCHOOL ACHIEVEMENTS
- Prefect
- Quidditch Keeper (Gryffindor)
- Special Award for Services to the School

66 'And what in the name of Merlin's most baggy Y Fronts was that about?' 99

66 'That's chess!' snapped Ron. 'You've got to make some sacrifices! I'll make my move and she'll take me — that leaves you free to checkmate the king, Harry!' 99

66 'Eat slugs, Malfoy.' 99

HOBBIES
Wizard chess and Quidditch

ERROL

SCABBERS

HERMIONE JEAN GRANGER

DATE OF BIRTH September 19, 1979   **HOGWARTS HOUSE** Gryffindor

ALSO KNOWN AS
Hermy *(Grawp)*
Know-it-all *(Ron Weasley)*
Miss Grant *(Professor Binns)*
Herm — own — ninny *(Viktor Krum)*

PARENTS
Mr. Granger (father, Muggle, dentist),
Mrs. Granger (mother, Muggle, dentist)

HOBBIES
Reading, studying, S.P.E.W. (Society for the Promotion of Elfish Welfare)

"'Me!' said Hermione. 'Books! And cleverness! There are more important things — friendship and bravery and — oh Harry — be *careful*!'"

Dumbledore's Army Galleon

"'Just because you've got the emotional range of a teaspoon doesn't mean we all have!'"

"'Wing-gar-dium Levi-o-sa . . .'"

PATRONUS
Otter

"'*Oppugno!*' came a shriek from the doorway. Harry spun around to see Hermione pointing her wand at Ron, her expression wild: The little flock of birds was speeding like a hail of fat golden bullets toward Ron . . .'"

"'We could all have been killed — or worse, expelled. Now, if you don't mind, I'm going to bed.'"

WAND
Dragon heartstring, vine, 10 ¾ inches

EYE COLOR
Brown

HOGWARTS: A History
SPELLMAN'S SYLLABARY

CROOKSHANKS

RULES HERMIONE HAS BROKEN AT HOGWARTS

- Entering the forbidden third-floor corridor
- Setting Professor Snape's robes on fire
- Smuggling an illegal dragon out of the school
- Brewing and using Polyjuice Potion
- Stealing potion ingredients from Professor Snape's personal cupboards
- Using the Disarming Charm on Professor Snape
- Trapping unregistered Animagus Rita Skeeter in a jar
- Creating (but not naming) Dumbledore's Army
- Using the Confundus Charm on Cormac McLaggen

Revealer

LUNA LOVEGOOD

DATE OF BIRTH February 13, 1981   **HOGWARTS HOUSE** Ravenclaw

❝ 'You're just as sane as I am.' ❞

HOBBIES
Reading
The Quibbler

Butterbeer cork necklace

Luna's roaring lion hat

26

❝ Luna was demonstrating her usual knack of speaking uncomfortable truths; he had never met anyone quite like her. ❞

PARENTS
Xenophilius Lovegood
(father, wizard, editor),
Pandora Lovegood
(mother, witch)

ALSO KNOWN AS
Loony Lovegood

MAGICAL ANIMALS LUNA BELIEVES IN

- ❧ Blibbering Humdingers
- ❧ Crumple-Horned Snorkacks
- ❧ Heliopaths
- ❧ Umgubular Slashkilters
- ❧ Nargles
- ❧ Aquavirius Maggots
- ❧ Wrackspurts
- ❧ Gulping Plimpies

HOME
The Lovegoods' house is a black, cylindrical building on top of a hill near the village of Ottery St. Catchpole, not far from the Burrow

EYE COLOR
Silver

❝ A Wrackspurt . . . They're invisible. They float in through your ears and make your brain go fuzzy.' ❞

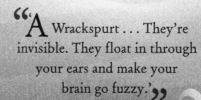

PATRONUS
Hare

NEVILLE LONGBOTTOM

DATE OF BIRTH July 30, 1980   **HOGWARTS HOUSE** Gryffindor

> 'Gran, I've lost my toad again.'

> 'It's a Remembrall! Gran knows I forget things — this tells you if there's something you've forgotten to do.'

BOGGART
Professor Snape

FAMILY
Frank Longbottom (father, wizard, Auror),
Alice Longbottom (mother, witch, Auror),
Augusta Longbottom (grandmother, witch)

WAND
Originally used his dad's old wand; Neville's second wand is unicorn hair and cherry

TREVOR

HOBBIES
Herbology

> 'There are all kinds of courage,' said Dumbledore, smiling. 'It takes a great deal of bravery to stand up to our enemies, but just as much to stand up to our friends. I therefore award ten points to Mr. Neville Longbottom.'

NEVILLE'S FIRST-YEAR MISHAPS

- Loses his toad, Trevor, while at platform nine and three-quarters
- Falls over on his way to the Sorting Hat's stool
- Runs across the Great Hall with the Sorting Hat still on his head
- Has a bundle of walking sticks dropped on his head by Peeves the poltergeist
- Melts Seamus Finnigan's cauldron
- Breaks his wrist after falling off his broom
- Has to bunny hop to Gryffindor Tower due to a Leg-Locker Curse
- Struck with a full Body-Bind Curse by Hermione Granger

RUBEUS HAGRID

DATE OF BIRTH December 6, 1928 **HOGWARTS HOUSE** Gryffindor

Rock cakes

> "'I would trust Hagrid with my life.'" — ALBUS DUMBLEDORE

HOME
Hagrid's hut

FOUND IN HAGRID'S POCKETS

- Handful of moldy dog-biscuits
- Gringotts vault key
- Bunches of keys
- Slug pellets
- Balls of string
- Mint humbugs
- Tea-bags
- Handful of Knuts and Galleons
- Squashy package of sausages
- A copper kettle
- A fire poker
- Teapot and chipped mugs
- A slightly squashed chocolate birthday cake
- A dirty spotted handkerchief
- A couple of dormice
- Rather ruffled-looking owl
- Quill
- Parchment
- Flowery pink umbrella

ALSO KNOWN AS

Keeper of Keys and Grounds at Hogwarts

Professor Hagrid (Care of Magical Creatures)

Hagger *(Grawp)*

WAND
Flowery pink umbrella (previously oak, 16 inches)

EYE COLOR
Black

FAMILY
Mr. Hagrid (father, wizard), **Fridwulfa** (mother, giantess), **Grawp** (half-brother, giant)

> "'Ah, well, people can be a bit stupid abou' their pets.'"

28

FANG

See some of Hagrid's pets on page 188 ➔

FAWKES

ALBUS PERCIVAL
WULFRIC BRIAN DUMBLEDORE

DATE OF BIRTH 1881 HOGWARTS HOUSE Gryffindor

"'NEVER —' he thundered, '— INSULT — ALBUS — DUMBLEDORE — IN — FRONT — OF — ME!'"

RUBEUS HAGRID

PARENTS

Percival Dumbledore
(father, wizard),
Kendra Dumbledore
(mother, witch)

SIBLINGS

Aberforth (brother,
wizard), **Ariana**
(sister, witch)

Deluminator

Lemon drops

"'Welcome to a new year at Hogwarts!
Before we begin our banquet, I would like
to say a few words. And here they are:
Nitwit! Blubber! Oddment! Tweak!
Thank you!'"

EYE COLOR

Blue

PATRONUS

Phoenix

Chocolate Frog Card

ENJOYS

- Chamber music
- Tenpin bowling
- Knitting patterns
- Lemon drops

ALBUS
DUMBLEDORE

"'It is our choices, Harry, that
show what we truly are, far more
than our abilities.'"

ACHIEVEMENTS INCLUDE

- Headmaster of Hogwarts
- Chocolate Frog Card
- Former Transfiguration teacher
- Order of Merlin, First Class
- Grand Sorcerer
- Chief Warlock of the Wizengamot
- Supreme Mugwump, International Confederation of Wizards
- Discovered twelve uses of dragon's blood
- Head Boy, Prefect, Winner of the Barnabus Finkley Prize for Exceptional Spell-Casting, British Youth Representative to the Wizengamot, Gold Medal-Winner for Ground-Breaking Contribution to the International Alchemical Conference in Cairo

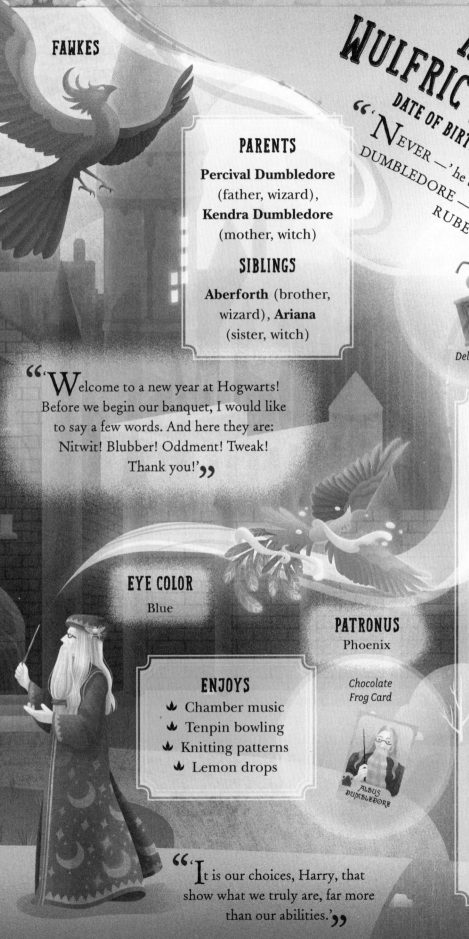

DRACO LUCIUS MALFOY

DATE OF BIRTH June 1980   **HOGWARTS HOUSE** Slytherin

"You don't know what I'm capable of. You don't know what I've done!"

SCHOOL ACHIEVEMENTS

- ♣ Quidditch Seeker (Slytherin)
- ♣ Inquisitorial Squad
- ♣ Prefect

HOME
Malfoy Manor

PARENTS
Lucius Malfoy
(father, wizard, Hogwarts school governor),
Narcissa Malfoy (mother, witch)

Vanishing Cabinet

ALSO KNOWN AS
The amazing bouncing ferret

Nimbus Two Thousand and One

EYE COLOR
Gray

"*Serpensortia!*"

WAND
Unicorn hair,
hawthorn, 10 inches

DRACO'S GREATEST INSULTS

"Honestly, if you were any slower, you'd be going backward.'

"Longbottom, if brains were gold you'd be poorer than Weasley, and that's saying something.'

"Imagine being in Hufflepuff, I think I'd leave, wouldn't you?'

"You'll soon find out some wizarding families are much better than others, Potter. You don't want to go making friends with the wrong sort. I can help you there.'

SEVERUS SNAPE

DATE OF BIRTH January 9, 1960   **HOGWARTS HOUSE** Slytherin

" 'Ah, yes . . . Harry Potter. Our new — celebrity.' "

PARENTS

Tobias Snape (father, Muggle),
Eileen Prince (mother, witch)

HOME

Spinner's End,
Cokeworth

EYE COLOR

Black

ALSO KNOWN AS

Snivellus
Sev

" 'Legilimens!' "

" 'What would I get if I added powdered root of asphodel to an infusion of wormwood?' "

ADVANCED POTION-MAKING
LIBATIUS BORAGE

TEACHING POSTS

- Potions master
- Head of Slytherin house
- Defense Against the Dark Arts teacher

" 'Yes, it is easy to see that nearly six years of magical education have not been wasted on you, Potter. Ghosts are transparent.' "

SPECIAL SKILLS

- Potions
- Occlumency
- Legilimency
- Defense Against the Dark Arts
- Logic

I AM LORD VOLDEMORT TOM MARVOLO RIDDLE

DATE OF BIRTH December 31, 1926 **HOGWARTS HOUSE** Slytherin

ALSO KNOWN AS
You-Know-Who, He-Who-Must-Not-Be-Named,
the Heir of Slytherin, the Dark Lord,
Tom Riddle

“'I fashioned myself a new
name, a name I knew
wizards everywhere would
one day fear to speak, when
I had become the greatest
sorcerer in the world!'”
TOM RIDDLE

School achievements

Borgin and Burkes

Borgin & Burkes

FAMILY

Tom Riddle Senior (father, Muggle),
Merope Riddle (mother, witch),
Morfin Gaunt (uncle, wizard),
Marvolo Gaunt (grandfather, wizard)

The graveyard, Little Hangleton

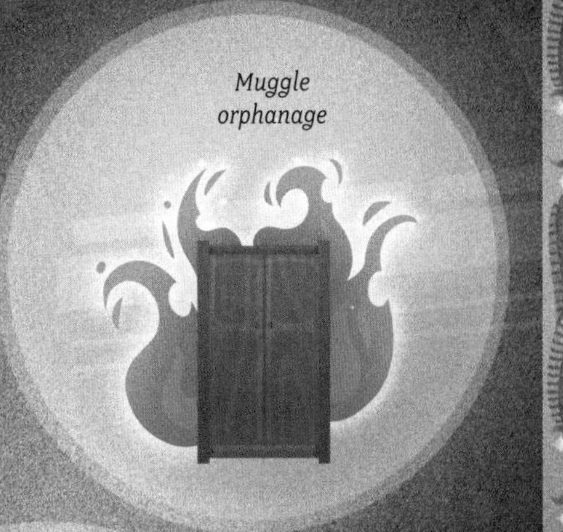

Muggle orphanage

The Riddle House, Little Hangleton

"*Avada Kedavra!*"

EYE COLOR
Scarlet

WAND
Phoenix tail feather, yew, 13½ inches

NAGINI

"How could they have believed I would not rise again? They, who knew the steps I took, long ago, to guard myself against mortal death? They, who had seen proofs of the immensity of my power in the times when I was mightier than any wizard living?"

33

GINNY WEASLEY

"'You think the dead we have loved ever truly leave us? You think that we don't recall them more clearly than ever in times of great trouble?'"

ALBUS DUMBLEDORE

"'The thing about growing up with Fred and George,' said Ginny thoughtfully, 'is that you sort of start thinking anything's possible if you've got enough nerve.'"

"Mrs. Weasley set the potion down on the bedside cabinet, bent down, and put her arms around Harry, and hugged him like this, as though by a mother."

He had no memory of ever being hugged like this, as though by a mother.

ARTHUR AND MOLLY WEASLEY

"'Go on, have a pasty,' said Harry, who had never had anything to share before or, indeed, anyone to share it with."

RON WEASLEY

"'Poor old Snuffles,' said Ron, breathing deeply. 'He must really like you, Harry. . . . Imagine having to live off rats.'"

SIRIUS BLACK

"'Wangoballwime?'
'Sorry?' said Cho.
'D'you want to go to the ball with me?' said Harry."

CHO C...

BEYOND
- THE -
REACH of MAGIC

NEVILLE LONGBOTTOM

"Harry felt in the pocket of his robes and pulled out a Chocolate Frog, the very last one from the box Hermione had given him for Christmas. He gave it to Neville, who looked as though he might cry."

SEVERUS SNAPE

"'Always,' said Snape."

"'After all this time?'"

"But from that moment on, Hermione Granger became their friend. There are some things you can't share without ending up liking each other, and knocking out a twelve-foot mountain troll is one of them."

HERMIONE GRANGER

"Of house-elves and children's tales, of love, loyalty, and innocence, Voldemort knows and understands nothing. Nothing. That they all have a power beyond his own, a power beyond the reach of any magic, is a truth he has never grasped."
ALBUS DUMBLEDORE

"Yes, Harry, you can love," said Dumbledore. . . . 'Which, given everything that has happened to you, is a great and remarkable thing.'"

HARRY POTTER

"Professor McGonagall sat down behind her desk, frowning at Harry. Then she said, 'Have a biscuit, Potter.'"

MINERVA McGONAGALL

"Should I ever asked me to a party before. 'Nobody's ever asked me to a party before, as a friend! Is that why you dyed your eyebrow, for the party?'"

"Oh, no, I'd love to go with you as friends!' said Luna, beaming as he had never seen her beam before, as a friend! Is that why you dyed your eyebrow, for the party?'"

LUNA LOVEGOOD

"Yeh know wha', Harry?' he said, looking up from the photograph of his father, his eyes very bright. 'When I firs' met you, you reminded me o' me a bit.'"

RUBEUS HAGRID

2

SPORTS, PEOPLE, AND EVERYTHING WIZARDING

(or S.P.E.W. for short)

Learn how magical folk evade Muggle eyes and take a peek at daily life for witches and wizards — from the essential practicalities of owl post and the Floo Network to the bustling pages of the *Daily Prophet*. Find out about magical means of travel, feast your eyes on sumptuous sweets and treats, admire curious clothing, and enjoy the esteemed sport of Quidditch. From broomsticks to Butterbeer, it's all waiting inside. . . .

Learn about more wizarding laws on page 163 ➡

CLOTHING GUIDELINES

WHEN MINGLING WITH MUGGLES, WIZARDS AND WITCHES WILL ADOPT AN ENTIRELY MUGGLE STANDARD OF DRESS

STATUTE OF – SECRECY –

NO EFFORT

HOW TO AVOID DISCOVERY

✥ PRACTICAL METHODS ✥

DON'T USE MAGIC *in Muggle areas*

Disguises

MISINFORMATION

Careful planning

✥ MAGICAL METHODS ✥

Muggle-Repelling Charms

Make areas unplottable
(so they're impossible to put on a map)

Concealment AND Disillusionment Charms

MEMORY AND CONFUNDUS CHARMS
(as backup if things go awry)

EVADING MUGGLE EYES

INTERNATIONAL CONFEDERATION OF WARLOCKS' STATUTE OF SECRECY

The wizarding community has many ways of keeping its secrets from Muggles, a practice going back centuries. Ever since 1692 the Statute of Secrecy has enforced strict guidelines, making it the law that the magical world stays completely hidden.

HALF-MAGICAL VILLAGES

Some villages have hidden wizarding communities. Notable examples are:

- Tinworth, Cornwall
- Upper Flagley, Yorkshire
- Ottery St. Catchpole, south coast of England
- Godric's Hollow, West Country

If precautions are taken, the Muggles will be none the wiser.*

The Confundus Charm can also help.

Spot more magical places on the map on page 66 ➡

38

> **Q**uidditch should not be played anywhere near any place where there is the slightest chance that a Muggle might be watching or we'll see how well you can play whilst chained to a dungeon wall.
>
> Wizards' Council Decree, 1419

BROOMSTICKS

Since medieval times broomsticks have been a means of flight that can easily be hidden in a house. Unfortunately Muggles have long associated witches with brooms, so extra caution is needed.

The One-Day Exception When Lord Voldemort disappeared after failing to kill the baby Harry Potter, the British wizarding community took to the streets to celebrate. They wore no disguises and Muggles noticed hundreds of owls flying in every direction in broad daylight.

MAGICAL BEASTS MUST STAY HIDDEN

EACH WIZARDING GOVERNING BODY WILL BE RESPONSIBLE FOR THE CONCEALMENT, CARE, AND CONTROL OF ALL MAGICAL BEASTS, BEINGS, AND SPIRITS DWELLING WITHIN ITS TERRITORY'S BORDERS.

~ Statute of Secrecy, Clause 73, 1750 ~

Famous Creature Sightings

- **Diricawl:** Muggles know it as the dodo and believe it's now extinct
- **Yeti:** Concealed by an International Task Force in the mountains
- **Kelpie:** One appears in sea serpent form in many photos, claimed to be fake
- **Snallygaster:** Has a dedicated Snallygaster Protection League
- **Hodag:** Muggles now think all sightings are hoaxes

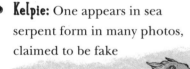

> **"T**he world's largest kelpie continues to evade capture in Loch Ness and appears to have developed a positive thirst for publicity.'**"**
>
> NEWT SCAMANDER, Magizoologist

TRAVELING UNSEEN

Wizards have no need for most Muggle technology. However, it's important that magical travel doesn't attract attention.

- **The Floo Network:** By traveling from fireplace to fireplace, wizards can move between buildings without setting foot outside
- **Portkeys:** These magical transportation devices can be made from ordinary objects, so they can be hidden in plain sight
- **Charmed vehicles:** Some wizards can't resist modifying cars; if, for example, they want to make one fly, it's a good idea to add a working Invisibility Booster

QUILLS AND STATIONERY

Wizarding writing tools can have helpful magical properties.

Detachable Cribbing Cuffs

EVERLASTING INK

Color-Change Ink

INVISIBLE INK

Self-Correcting Ink

Roonil Wazlib

Anti-Cheating Quill
Given to first years for exams

Auto-Answer Quill
Banned in O.W.L. exams

Self-Inking, Spell-Checking, Smart-Answer Quill
Sold at Weasleys' Wizard Wheezes

Quick-Quotes Quill
Lets Rita Skeeter write while keeping her hands free

Deluxe Sugar Quill
Disguised sweets you can enjoy in class

Spellotape
Sticks objects together; not useful for repairing wands

Revealer
Sold in Diagon Alley and is meant to reveal invisible ink

The Quill of Acceptance
Writes the names of students accepted into Hogwarts

Luxury quills can be made from eagle, pheasant, or peacock feathers. The magical bird the Fwooper also offers feathers for fancy quills.

EVERYDAY MAGIC

" 'I don't know how the Muggles manage without magic.' "

RUBEUS HAGRID

HOWLERS

Howlers are a more dramatic way of sending a message. They're identifiable by their scarlet envelopes. Upon delivery a Howler begins to smoke, then, delivers its message in a roar of sound, and finally bursts into flame. If you don't open one right away, it explodes.

" 'All those substitutes for magic Muggles use — electricity, computers, and radar, and all those things — they all go haywire around Hogwarts, there's too much magic in the air.' "

HERMIONE GRANGER

COOKING

" 'She tapped the pot again; it rose into the air, flew toward Harry, and tipped over; Mrs. Weasley slid a bowl neatly beneath it just in time to catch the stream of thick, steaming onion soup. "

Food is one of the five Principal Exceptions to Gamp's Law of Elemental Transfiguration.

" 'It's impossible to make good food out of nothing! You can Summon it if you know where it is, you can transform it, you can increase the quantity if you've already got some —' "

HERMIONE GRANGER

A Cauldron Full of Hot, Strong Love

Oh, come and stir my cauldron,

And if you do it right,

I'll boil you up some hot, strong love

To keep you warm tonight.

"We danced to this when we were eighteen!' said Mrs. Weasley, wiping her eyes on her knitting. 'Do you remember, Arthur?'"

MAGICAL PAINTINGS

Artists enchant their paintings, allowing them to move and speak. A portrait's ability to interact with the real world is determined by the power of the witch or wizard who was painted.

CELESTINA WARBECK

"The old radio next to the sink had just announced that coming up was 'Witching Hour, with the popular singing sorceress, Celestina Warbeck.'"

ENTERTAINMENT

WIZARD CHESS

"This was exactly like Muggle chess except that the figures were alive, which made it a lot like directing troops in battle."

"'Don't send me there, can't you see his knight? Send him, we can afford to lose him.'
RON WEASLEY"

EXPLODING SNAP

"Ron was busy building a card castle out of his Exploding Snap pack — a much more interesting pastime than with Muggle cards, because of the chance that the whole thing would blow up at any second."

The chess pieces can talk back to the players

GOBSTONES

An ancient two-player game. Each player has fifteen Gobstones (small, round balls made of stone or precious metals) and must capture all the opposing stones.

The stones squirt a foul-smelling liquid as a penalty for capture.

BROOM GAMES

The most popular sport is Quidditch but there are many other games involving flying. One children's game is Shuntbumps, where players try to knock each other off their brooms.

Self-Shuffling playing cards

Learn about Quidditch on page 60 ➜

41

COMMUNICATION

DAILY PROPHET
The only wizarding newspaper in Britain is delivered every morning all over the country.

EVENING PROPHET
This evening edition of the *Daily Prophet* comes out if something unusually interesting happens.

THE QUIBBLER
The magazine is published every month and used by some as a questionable news source.

RADIO
The radio is a rare piece of Muggle technology that's legally modified and used in daily wizarding life. Many households listen to the Wizarding Wireless Network (WWN).

REPORTED NEWS

PHOENIX MAGIC
Some intelligent and loyal pets can act as messengers. Fawkes has been known to leave behind a single feather as a warning.

> "There was a flash of flame in the very middle of the office, leaving behind a single golden feather that floated gently to the floor."

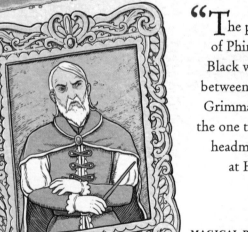

> "The painted image of Phineas Nigellus Black was able to flit between his portrait in Grimmauld Place and the one that hung in the headmaster's office at Hogwarts."

MAGICAL PORTRAITS
Portraits not only speak, but can move between paintings. If a witch or wizard has a portrait in more than one place, they can make a useful messenger.

ENCHANTING MESSENGERS

OWL POST
The most common means of communication in the wizarding world. Owls will deliver letters, newspapers, and packages wherever they can fly. They can make both local and overseas deliveries.

> "There were delays in the post because the owls kept being blown off course."

Find out how Hermione uses the Protean Charm on page 129 ➡

FLOO POWDER

The Floo Network lets people speak face-to-face. After throwing Floo powder into a fireplace, you can make your head appear in someone else's fireplace and speak with them.

For more on the Floo Network, go to page 48 ➡

TWO-WAY MIRRORS

CHARMED DEVICES

INTER-DEPARTMENTAL MEMOS

In the Ministry of Magic, departments send messages to each other using paper memos, which are charmed to fly around the building. They used to use owls but the mess was unbelievable.

"This is a two-way mirror. I've got the other. If you need to speak to me, just say my name into it; you'll appear in my mirror and I'll be able to talk in yours. James and I used to use them when we were in separate detentions."

SIRIUS BLACK

PROTEAN CHARM

This charm makes separate objects mimic each other. If a message is added to one, it will appear on all the others no matter where they are. Students have used it to turn small items such as coins into secret communication devices.

MAGICAL CONVERSATIONS

PATRONUSES

The Patronus Charm creates a Patronus, a magical guardian in the shape of an animal. It can travel and speak a message in its caster's voice.

Only Order of the Phoenix members use their Patronuses in this way, with teaching from Albus Dumbledore, who came up with the idea.

"If anyone gets in trouble, send up red sparks, an' we'll all come an' find yeh.'"

RUBEUS HAGRID

MAGICAL SPARK SIGNALS

Wands can send sparks into the sky in different colors.

FLAGRATE!
This spell lets you place a magical mark on something.

SPELLS AND SIGNALS

THE DARK MARK

The Dark Mark is a symbol of a skull with a snake protruding from its mouth.

Lord Voldemort's followers, the Death Eaters, make the Dark Mark appear in the sky to reveal where they have been.

Death Eaters are branded with the Dark Mark on their left arm. Lord Voldemort summons them by making their brands burn.

43

Discover more about the Order of the Phoenix on page 174 ➡

Scops owl

> "**P**igwidgeon plummeted twelve feet before managing to pull himself back up again; the letter attached to his leg was much longer and heavier than usual. . . ."

THE OWLMANAC

POST OWLS

Owls have an uncanny ability to deliver letters to anyone wherever they are, even when given a name with no address.

It is safe to assume that almost every owl you see is a post owl working for an individual or the Owl Postal Service.

While owls can reliably and quickly track someone down, it takes powerful magic to avoid receiving letters from them, requiring Repelling, Disguising, or Masking Spells.

44

> "'**E**rrol!' said Ron, pulling the bedraggled owl out by the feet."

Great gray owl

Tawny (or brown) owl

MESSENGER PETS

Trained post owls are highly valued. They make popular pets, although they're expensive and many families will share an owl or borrow one from the postal service.

Little owl

O.W.L.S

Ordinary Wizarding Levels (O.W.L.s) are not birds, but exams that Hogwarts students take in their fifth year. Harry, Ron, and Hermione's results are delivered by three handsome tawny owls.

THE OWLERY

At Hogwarts students keep their pet owls in the Owlery, a circular stone room with perches that rise right up to the ceiling. It houses hundreds of owls, with the pets sitting alongside school owls that anyone can borrow.

See who has which pet owl on page 178 ➤

Snowy owl

Eagle owl

OWL TREATS

Owls hunt for food at night, and will sometimes bring back mice, voles, and frogs. Owners can also give them Owl Treats or buy boxes of owl nuts from Eeylops Owl Emporium.

THE AMAZING FLIGHTS OF HEDWIG

Hedwig never fails to find her way somewhere. She . . .

- Flies from Hogwarts to Romania to deliver a letter to Charlie Weasley

- Takes a letter from Privet Drive to an unknown country with tropical birds, where Sirius is hiding

- Travels to France to collect Harry's birthday present from Hermione

- Delivers letters to Sirius while he's on the run from Dementors

- Shows up at the Leaky Cauldron five minutes after Harry arrives on the Knight Bus

- Finds Ron and Hermione at Grimmauld Place and follows Harry's instructions to keep pecking them if they don't send him long replies

Barn owl

45

Screech owl

BREAKFAST IN THE GREAT HALL

"It had given him a bit of a shock on the first morning, when about a hundred owls had suddenly streamed into the Great Hall during breakfast, circling the tables until they saw their owners, and dropping letters and packages onto their laps."

Hedwig has unusual taste for an owl and sometimes likes to share Harry's breakfast. While visiting the Gryffindor table she's tried:

- Orange juice • A bit of toast
- Bacon rinds • Neville's cornflakes

"The snowy owl clicked her beak and nibbled his ear affectionately. . . ."

DAILY PROPHET DELIVERY OWLS

Owls who deliver the *Daily Prophet* collect payment in a leather pouch. Hermione's subscription costs one Knut per newspaper.

The *Daily Prophet* also advertises products you can buy by owl-order.

Find a list of special owl deliveries on page 206 ➔

DAILY PROPHET

EDITOR
BARNABAS CUFFE

WIZARDING

Dumbledore

INQUIRY AT THE MINISTRY

ARTHUR WEASLEY, Artifacts Office, bewitching a Muggle ca

Mr. Lucius Malfoy, Witchcraft and Wizard earlier this year, called

"Weasley has brou into disrepute," Mr Ma "He is clearly unfit laws and his ridicu Act should be scrap

FURTHER MISTAKES
—AT THE—
MINISTRY OF MAGIC

IT SEEMS AS the Minist Magic's troub not yet at a writes Rita Special Corres Recently und for its poor control at the Quidditch Cup, and still unable to a for the disappearance of one witches, the Ministry was pl into fresh embarrassment yes by the antics of Arnold W

MINISTRY OF MAGIC EMPLOYEE SCOOPS GRAND PRIZE

ARTHUR WEASLEY, HEAD O Misuse of M at an Gal

A Prop on a our break

The a mon start Hogwar the W attend.

BLACK S

PO int be , is Min day. capt Mag in

SCENES OF TERROR
AT THE QUIDDITCH WORLD CUP

If the terrified wizards and witc breathlessly for news at the edg expected reassurance from the M they were sadly disappointed. A they emerged some time after the a Dark Mark, alleging that nobo but refusing to give any more in this statement will be enough that several bodies were remov

"I suppose I get my strength fro parents. I know they'd be very proud o they could see me now. . . . Yes, some night I still cry about them, I'm not to admit it. . . . I know nothing will during the tournament, because watching over me. . . ."

Harry has at last found love at His close friend, Colin Creeve Harry is rarely seen out of the one Hermione Granger, a stumm born girl who, like Harry, is one of the

HA
"DIST

THE BO He-Wh Named is u dangerous, *Correspondent.* recently come

NEWS

Giant Mistake

ALBUS DUMBLEDORE, ECCENTRIC headmaster of Hogwarts School [of] Witchcraft and Wizardry, [ha]s never been afraid to make [con]troversial staff appointments, [wri]tes *Rita Skeeter, Special Correspondent.* [In] September of this year, he hired [Profes]tor "Mad-Eye" Moody, the notoriously [jinx]-happy ex-Auror, to teach Defense [aga]inst the Dark Arts, a decision that [rai]sed many raised eyebrows at the [Minist]ry of Magic, given Moody's well-[...] of attacking anybody [...] [move]ment in his [...]

[...]L AT LARGE

[HAR]RY POTTER

[DISTURB]ED AND DANGEROUS"

[...] DEFEATED [You-Know-Who] [...] N o t - B e - [...] [coul]d possibly

[S]keeter, *Special* [e]vidence has [ab]out H[arry] Potter that All[...]

"He might even be pretending," said one specialist. "This could be a plea for attention."

The *Daily Prophet*, however, has unearthed worrying facts about Harry Potter that[...]

editor: Xenophilius Lovegood

THE QUIBBLER

crumple-Horned Snorkack sighting?

Sirius — black as He's painted?
Notorious mass murderer or innocent singing sensation?

For fourteen years Sirius Black has been believed guilty of the mass murder of twelve innocent Muggles and one wizard. Black's audacious escape from Azkaban two years ago has led to the widest manhunt ever conducted by the Ministry of Magic. None of us has ever questioned that he deserves to be recaptured and handed back to the Dementors.

[Qui]dditch League: How the Tornados are taking control

If you[...] the runes[...] heads the[...] a spell to[...] enemy's [...] into kum[...]

The Tutshi[ll...] were winning[...] League [...] a co[...] [...]ille[...] [...]nd[...]

[...] wizard who claim[ed] [to h]ave flown to the mo[on] [...] on a Cleansweep Six [...] brought back a bag [of] [...] moon frogs to prove[...]

Harry potter speaks out at Last:
-but does he?
[The tr]uth about[...]

Sources close to the Minister have recently disclosed that Fudge's dearest ambition is to seize control of the goblin gold supplies an[d...] that he will not hesitate to use force if need be. "It wouldn't be the first time, either," [said...] "Cornelius 'Goblin-Crusher' Fud[ge...] you could hear him wh[...] talking ab[...]

True forerunner of the racing broom ↓

SILVER ARROW

Madam Hooch learned to fly on a Silver Arrow ↓

Flies up to 70 miles an hour with a tailwind

COMET

Both Cho and Tonks fly a Comet 260 ↓

Draco owns a Comet 260, among other brooms ↓

In 1929, Falmouth Falcons players Randolph Keitch and Basil Horton established the Comet Trading Company ↑

Their first broom was the Comet 140, with a patented Horton–Keitch Braking Charm ↑

BROOMSTICKS

"There were the two large broom-shaped holes in Umbridge's office door, through which Fred and George's Cleansweeps had smashed to rejoin their masters."

CLEANSWEEP

In 1926, brothers Bob, Bill, and Barnaby Ollerton started the Cleansweep Broom Company →

Fred and George fly Cleansweep Fives; Ron later flies a Cleansweep Eleven

The first model, the Cleansweep One, was an instant success

The Quibbler interviewed a wizard who claimed to have flown to the moon on a Cleansweep Six and brought back a bag of moon frogs to prove it ↓

THE FLOO NETWORK

48

Travel on the Floo Network is via wizarding fireplaces.

Connections to the Network are made by the Ministry of Magic's Floo Regulation Panel.

This stops Muggle fireplaces accidentally joining up (although temporary connections are possible).

For more on the Floo Network, go to page 43 ⚡

Travelers throw a pinch of Floo powder into the fire.

The flames turn emerald green, then the traveler steps into the fire and shouts where they wish to go.

It's important to speak clearly and get out at the right grate.

Floo powder was invented by Ignatia Wildsmith in the thirteenth century. Its manufacture is strictly controlled.

The only licensed producer in Britain is Floo-Pow, a company whose headquarters is in Diagon Alley, and who never answer their front door.

No shortage of Floo powder has ever been reported. Its price has remained constant for one hundred years: two Sickles a scoop.

MAGICAL

PORTKEYS

Portkeys are everyday Muggle objects that have been bewitched with the incantation "*Portus*." They can transport wizards from one spot to another at a prearranged time.

When an object is turned into a Portkey, it glows blue. It also glows blue when it's time to travel.

Portkeys can transport large groups at a time. There were two hundred Portkeys placed at strategic points around Britain for the 1994 Quidditch World Cup.

"What sort of objects are Portkeys?' said Harry curiously. 'Well, they can be anything,' said Mr. Weasley. 'Unobtrusive things, obviously, so Muggles don't go picking them up and playing with them . . . stuff they'll just think is litter. . . .'"

THE HOGWARTS EXPRESS

HOGWARTS EXPRESS

Hogwarts students travel to school by train, departing from King's Cross, platform nine and three-quarters.

Find a ticket on page 86 →

SHOOTING STAR

In 1955, Universal Brooms Ltd. introduced the Shooting Star, the cheapest racing broom to date

"Ron's old Shooting Star was often outstripped by passing butterflies."

State-of-the-art racing broom, used by the Irish team in the 1994 Quidditch World Cup

"The Firebolt turned with the lightest touch; it seemed to obey his thoughts rather than his grip."

After an initial burst of popularity, it was found to lose speed and height as it aged

Streamlined, super-fine handle of ash, treated with diamond-hard polish

Hand-numbered with its own registration number

FIREBOLT

NIMBUS

Universal Brooms went out of business in 1978

Hogwarts school brooms include the Shooting Star

In 1967, the Nimbus Racing Broom Company was formed

Lucius Malfoy bought Nimbus 2001 brooms for Draco and the whole of the Slytherin Quidditch team in Harry's second year

Harry's first broomstick was a Nimbus 2000, a present from Professor McGonagall

The Nimbus 1000 flies up to 100 miles an hour, and can turn 360 degrees at a fixed point in midair

Acceleration of 0–150 miles an hour in ten seconds with an Unbreakable Braking Charm

Harry was given a Firebolt in his third year at Hogwarts

MEANS OF TRAVEL

There are many everyday ways to travel through the wizarding world, such as by broomstick, Apparition, or via the Floo Network. More unusual ways include by dragon, Thestral, or flying motorbike.

APPARITION

● Once a witch or wizard turns seventeen, they may take Apparition lessons and must then pass a test with the Department of Magical Transportation

● Apparators first fix their mind on a location, then disappear and reappear in that place

● There are three Ds to remember when Apparating: destination, determination, and deliberation

● Apparition is increasingly unreliable over very long distances, and only highly skilled wizards should attempt it across continents

● Side-Along-Apparition can be used when an Apparator travels with a companion, for example an underage wizard

● The most common injury from Apparition is Splinching — the separation of random body parts — which may require help from the Accidental Magic Reversal Squad

● Most wizarding dwellings are magically protected from unwanted Apparators; for example, it is not possible to Apparate anywhere inside the grounds of Hogwarts

MORE UNUSUAL FORMS OF TRANSPORT

● Flying car
● Flying motorbike
● Dragon ● Thestral
● Phoenix ● Centaur
● Beauxbatons carriage
● Vanishing Cabinet
● Durmstrang ship
● Toilet network
● Time-Turner

THE KNIGHT BUS

Ideal for a stranded witch or wizard in need of emergency transport.

● Learn more on page 50 ➜

NIGHT DAY

The Knight Bus is driven by Ernie Prang and the conductor is Stan Shunpike.

There are seats during the day and brass bedsteads at night.

"You keepin' well, then, 'Arry? I seen your name in the paper loads over the summer, but it weren't never nuffink very nice. I said to Ern, I said, "'e didn't seem like a nutter when we met 'im, just goes to show, dunnit?'"
STAN SHUNPIKE

50

ELEVEN SICKLES

CHILD SINGLE
FROM: Grimmauld Place London
TO: Hogwarts School of Witchcraft and Wizardry

THE KNIGHT BUS

If a witch or wizard is in urgent need of transport,
they can raise their wand arm at a street curb
and the Knight Bus will appear.

'Welcome to the Knight Bus, emergency transport for the stranded witch or wizard. Just stick out your wand hand, step on board, and we can take you anywhere you want to go.'
STAN SHUNPIKE

''E's 'Arry Potter! I can see 'is scar!'
STAN SHUNPIKE

It can travel anywhere on land, but not underwater.

It can be a bumpy ride; hot drinks are available, but not always advisable.

51

Minister of Magic Dugald McPhail introduced the Knight Bus in 1865.

'Listen, how much would it be to get to London?' 'Eleven Sickles,' said Stan, 'but for fifteen you get 'ot chocolate, and for fifteen you get an 'ot-water bottle an' a toofbrush in the color of your choice.'

THIRTEEN SICKLES
CHILD SINGLE
FROM: Magnolia Crescent, Little Whinging
TO: Diagon Alley & hot chocolate

'BANG. A violently purple, triple-decker bus had appeared out of thin air in front of them.'

FANTASTIC TREATS

STRAWBERRY

BAKED BEANS

COCONUT

TOAST

SPROUT

THE TROLLEY ON THE HOGWARTS EXPRESS

Chocolate Frogs

Pumpkin Pasties

Cauldron Cakes

CURRY

Pumpkin juice

Licorice Wands

ALBUS DUMBLEDORE, currently headmaster of Hogwarts. Considered by many the greatest wizard of modern times, Professor Dumbledore is particularly famous for his defeat of the Dark wizard Grindelwald in 1945, for the discovery of the twelve uses of dragon's blood, and his work on alchemy with his partner, Nicolas Flamel. Professor Dumbledore enjoys chamber music and tenpin bowling.

TEA WITH HAGRID

Tea

"Beef" casserole

Stoat sandwiches

Rock cakes

Treacle toffee

Dandelion juice

Drooble's **BEST Blowing Gum**

52

COFFEE

Professor McGonagall's Ginger Newt Biscuits

FRED AND GEORGE'S INVENTIONS

"'Have a biscuit, Potter.'"

Puking Pastilles

Ton-Tongue Toffee

Edible Dark Marks

Fainting Fancies

ZONKO'S Hiccup SWEETS

Nosebleed Nougat

Blood Blisterpods

THE HOGWARTS TABLE

GRASS

Sausages

BREAKFAST

Coffee

Pumpkin juice

Mashed potatoes

Ketchup

Bacon

Fried eggs

Porridge

Tea

Yorkshire pudding

Fried tomatoes

Milk jug

Marmalade

Chicken casserole

Toast

Kippers

Sugar bowl

Roast beef

SARDINE

PEPPER

BOGEY

MARMALADE

THE TRIWIZARD TOURNAMENT FEAST

"The Tournament will be officially opened at the end of the feast,' said Dumbledore. 'I now invite you all to eat, drink, and make yourselves at home!'"

CELEBRATIONS

EASTER EGGS

"Harry's and Ron's were the size of dragon eggs and full of homemade toffee."

54

AFTER THE FIRST TASK

"Sure enough, when they entered the Gryffindor common room it exploded with cheers and yells. . . ."

BILL AND FLEUR'S WEDDING

"A shower of silver stars fell upon them, spiraling around their now entwined figures."

HARRY'S BIRTHDAY DINNER

"'Seventeen, eh!' said Hagrid as he accepted a bucket-sized glass of wine from Fred. 'Six years ter the day since we met, Harry, d'yeh remember it?' 'Vaguely,' said Harry, grinning up at him. 'Didn't you smash down the front door, give Dudley a pig's tail, and tell me I was a wizard?'"

HARRY'S FIRST CHRISTMAS AT HOGWARTS

"It had been Harry's best Christmas day ever."

THE YULE BALL

"The walls of the Hall had all been covered in sparkling silver frost, with hundreds of garlands of mistletoe and ivy crossing the starry black ceiling. The House tables had vanished; instead, there were about a hundred smaller, lantern-lit ones, each seating about a dozen people."

CHRISTMAS AT GRIMMAULD PLACE

"They heard Sirius tramping past their door toward Buckbeak's room, singing 'God Rest Ye Merry, Hippogriffs'...."

Albus Dumbledore

Rita Skeeter

Sybill Trelawney

Dolores Umbridge

Minerva McGonagall

A CURIOUS COLLECTION OF CLOTHING

Hogwarts School of Witchcraft and Wizardry

Beauxbatons Academy of Magic

Durmstrang Institute

SCHOOL UNIFORMS

Harry Potter

Ron Weasley

Hermione Granger

Draco Malfoy

Fleur Delacour

Pansy Parkinson

Rubeus Hagrid

Minerva McGonagall

THE YULE BALL

Parvati Patil

Padma Patil

Quirinus Quirrell

Gilderoy Lockhart

Cornelius Fudge

Augusta Longbottom

Rubeus Hagrid

WEASLEY FAMILY JUMPERS

"'Why aren't you wearing yours, Ron?' George demanded. 'Come on, get it on, they're lovely and warm.'
'I hate maroon,' Ron moaned halfheartedly as he pulled it over his head.
'You haven't got a letter on yours,' George observed. 'I suppose she thinks you don't forget your name. But we're not stupid — we know we're called Gred and Forge.'"

Fred and George

Ron

Harry

Dobby

Percy

DOBBY THE HOUSE-ELF

The wizarding world has a lot of unique sayings, which regularly come up in conversation.

"I'm only yanking your wand, I'm Fred really —"
FRED WEASLEY

"Well, it's no good crying over spilled potion, I suppose . . . but the cat's among the pixies now."
ARABELLA FIGG

"Poisonous toadstools don't change their spots."
RON WEASLEY

SAYINGS AND

"Gallopin' Gorgons, that reminds me," said Hagrid, clapping a hand to his forehead with enough force to knock over a cart horse.

"One of those superstitions, isn't it? "May-born witches will marry Muggles." "Jinx by twilight, undone by midnight." "Wand of elder, never prosper." You must've heard them. My mum's full of them.'
RON WEASLEY

"And what in the name of Merlin's most baggy Y Fronts was that about?"
RON WEASLEY

"Old Dodgy Doge can get off his high hippogriff, because I've had access to a source most journalists would swap their wands for."
RITA SKEETER

"Merlin's beard," Moody whispered, staring at the map, his magical eye going haywire. "This . . . this is some map, Potter!"

"Another Weasley? You breed like gnomes."
AUNTIE MURIEL

"Time is Galleons, little brother."
FRED WEASLEY

"Don't count your owls before they are delivered," said Dumbledore gravely. "Which, now I think of it, ought to be some time later today."

SUPERSTITIONS

1 OMENS

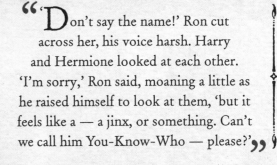

"'The Grim, my dear, the Grim!' cried Professor Trelawney, who looked shocked that Harry hadn't understood. 'The giant, spectral dog that haunts churchyards! My dear boy, it is an omen — the worst omen — of *death*!'"

FAIRY TALES 2

"'There were once three brothers who were *traveling along a lonely, winding road at twilight* —' 'Midnight, our mum always told us,' said Ron, who had stretched out, arms behind his head, to listen. Hermione shot him a look of annoyance. 'Sorry, I just think it's a bit spookier if it's midnight!' said Ron. 'Yeah, because we really need a bit more fear in our lives,' said Harry before he could stop himself."

"'Those are the Deathly Hallows,' said Xenophilius. He picked up a quill from a packed table at his elbow, and pulled a torn piece of parchment from between more books. 'The Elder Wand,' he said, and he drew a straight vertical line upon the parchment. 'The Resurrection Stone,' he said, and he added a circle on top of the line. 'The Cloak of Invisibility,' he finished, enclosing both line and circle in a triangle, to make the symbol that so intrigued Hermione. 'Together,' he said, 'the Deathly Hallows.'"

3 TABOO

"'Don't say the name!' Ron cut across her, his voice harsh. Harry and Hermione looked at each other. 'I'm sorry,' Ron said, moaning a little as he raised himself to look at them, 'but it feels like a — a jinx, or something. Can't we call him You-Know-Who — please?'"

4 CONSPIRACY

"'The Aurors are part of the Rotfang Conspiracy, I thought everyone knew that. They're working to bring down the Ministry of Magic from within using a combination of Dark Magic and gum disease.'"

LUNA LOVEGOOD

5 SECOND SIGHT

"'Would anyone like me to help them interpret the shadowy portents within their Orb?' she murmured over the clinking of her bangles. 'I don't need help,' Ron whispered. 'It's obvious what this means. There's going to be loads of fog tonight.'"

6 SUPERSTITION

"'If I join the table, we shall be thirteen! Nothing could be more unlucky! Never forget that when thirteen dine together, the first to rise will be the first to die!' 'We'll risk it, Sybill,' said Professor McGonagall impatiently. 'Do sit down, the turkey's getting stone cold.'"

NUMEROLOGY 7

"'Isn't seven the most powerfully magical number . . . ?'"

QUIDDITCH

TRIVIA

There are thirteen teams in the British and Irish League. The oldest is Puddlemere United, founded in 1163.

❧

The Dangerous Dai Commemorative Medal is awarded every season to the player who has taken the most exciting and foolhardy risks during a game.

❧

In 1884 a game on Bodmin Moor lasted for six months when neither Seeker could catch the Snitch.

❧

The first rule of Brutus Scrimgeour's *The Beaters' Bible* is "Take out the Seeker."

❧

The British record for the fastest capture of a Snitch is three and a half seconds, made by Roderick Plumpton of the Tutshill Tornados.

60

> "It's our sport. Wizard sport. It's like — like soccer in the Muggle world — everyone follows Quidditch — played up in the air on broomsticks and there's four balls — sorta hard ter explain the rules."

RUBEUS HAGRID

QUIDDITCH BALLS

QUAFFLE
Leather, 12 inches

- Gripping Charm; bewitched so it falls slowly if dropped
- Chasers throw it through the hoops to gain 10 points
- The Keeper guards the goalposts

GOLDEN SNITCH
Metal, walnut-sized

- Bewitched to evade capture and to stay on the pitch
- The Seeker must catch it to gain 150 points and end the game

BLUDGER x 2
Iron, 10 inches

- Bewitched to chase and attack the closest player
- Beaters use their bats to knock the Bludgers away from their team

> "Oh, you wait, it's the best game in the world —"

RON WEASLEY

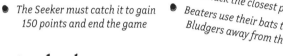

Keeper

Chasers

Beaters

Seeker

Players may fly as high as they want above the pitch, as long as they don't cross the boundary lines

THE PITCH

CENTRAL CIRCLE
For releasing the balls

GOALPOSTS
Three per side

SCORING AREA
Only one Chaser is allowed here at a time

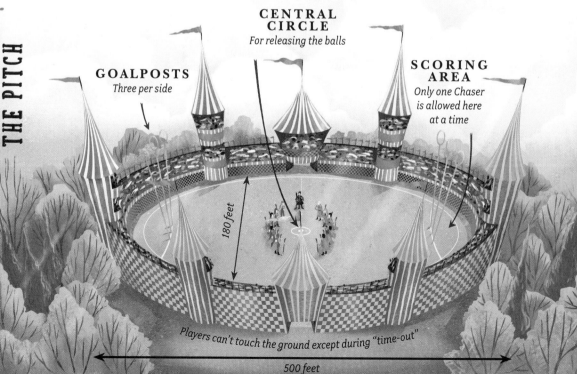

180 feet

Players can't touch the ground except during "time-out"

500 feet

HOW TO GET THERE

Arrivals were staggered to avoid Muggle suspicion. People with cheaper tickets had to arrive two weeks beforehand.

MUGGLE TRANSPORT

Train and bus travel were allowed for a limited number of people.

APPARITION

Wizards could Apparate to an Apparition point in a nearby wood, where Muggles wouldn't see them appearing.

PORTKEYS

Two hundred Portkeys were placed at strategic points all around Britain.

WHERE TO STAY

World Cup spectators stayed at a Muggle campsite close to the stadium.

Visitors had to set up tents the Muggle way, without using magic

THE 1994 QUIDDITCH WORLD CUP

The final took place in Dartmoor, England. A hundred thousand wizards from all over the world came to watch the match between Ireland and Bulgaria.

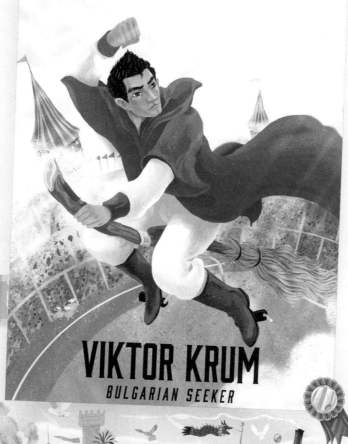

VIKTOR KRUM
BULGARIAN SEEKER

MATCH HIGHLIGHTS

HAWKSHEAD ATTACKING FORMATION
Three Irish Chasers zoom closely together in an arrowhead shape, bearing down upon the Bulgarians.

PORSKOFF PLOY
An Irish Chaser darts upward with the Quaffle to draw away a Bulgarian player, but then drops the ball down to a teammate.

WRONSKI FEINT
The Seeker dives at full speed toward the ground, tricking the other Seeker into following. Krum successfully pulls off this dangerous diversion, making the Irish Seeker crash.

"Harry turned this way and that, staring through his Omnioculars, as the Quaffle changed hands with the speed of a bullet."

SOUVENIRS

- Luminous rosettes that squeal the names of the players
- Collectable figures of famous players
- Irish and Bulgarian flags that play the national anthems when waved
- Tiny model Firebolts
- Pointed green hats bedecked with dancing shamrocks
- Bulgarian scarves adorned with roaring lions
- Omnioculars

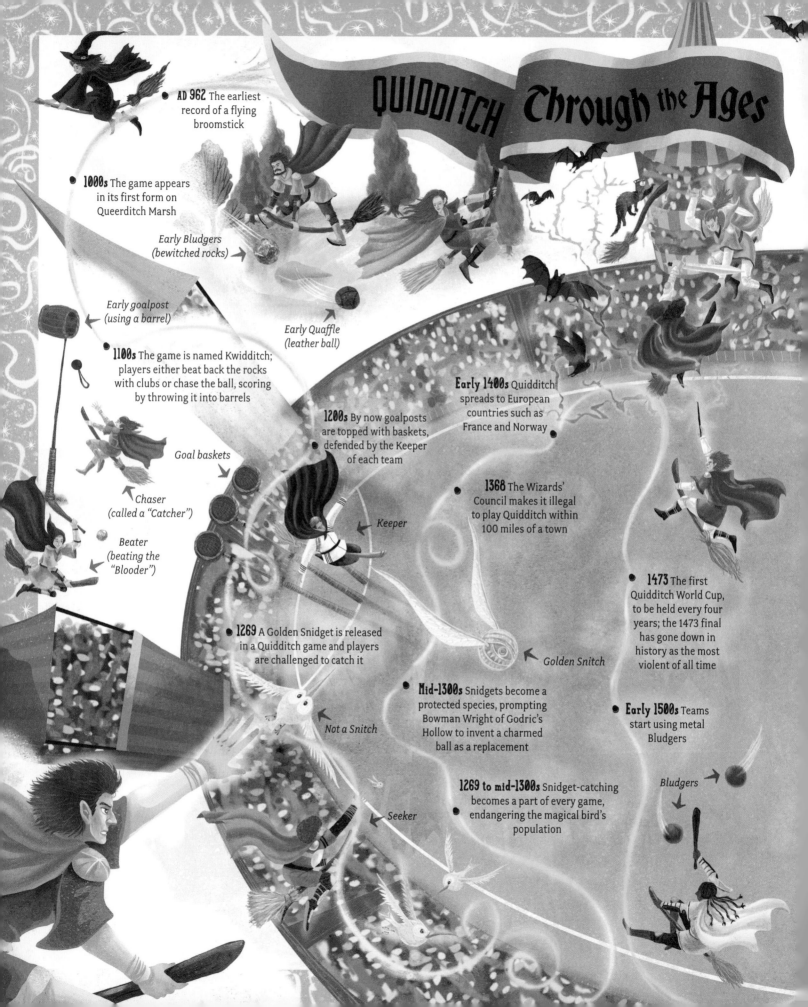

QUIDDITCH Through the Ages

AD 962 The earliest record of a flying broomstick

1000s The game appears in its first form on Queerditch Marsh

Early Bludgers (bewitched rocks)

Early goalpost (using a barrel)

Early Quaffle (leather ball)

1100s The game is named Kwidditch; players either beat back the rocks with clubs or chase the ball, scoring by throwing it into barrels

Goal baskets

Chaser (called a "Catcher")

Beater (beating the "Blooder")

1200s By now goalposts are topped with baskets, defended by the Keeper of each team

Keeper

Early 1400s Quidditch spreads to European countries such as France and Norway

1368 The Wizards' Council makes it illegal to play Quidditch within 100 miles of a town

1473 The first Quidditch World Cup, to be held every four years; the 1473 final has gone down in history as the most violent of all time

1269 A Golden Snidget is released in a Quidditch game and players are challenged to catch it

Not a Snitch

Golden Snitch

Mid-1300s Snidgets become a protected species, prompting Bowman Wright of Godric's Hollow to invent a charmed ball as a replacement

Early 1500s Teams start using metal Bludgers

1269 to mid-1300s Snidget-catching becomes a part of every game, endangering the magical bird's population

Bludgers

Seeker

1692 The Department of Magical Games and Sports starts enforcing Statute of Secrecy guidelines

1711 The Quaffle becomes scarlet for better visibility; shortly after this, Daisy Pennifold invents the modern version of the ball

Pennifold Quaffle

1750 The Department of Magical Games and Sports sets down the standard Quidditch rules

1877 The Tournament that Nobody Remembers: All memories of this year's World Cup go missing, although some players are left with mysterious injuries; a replacement tournament is held in 1878

1674 Formation of the British and Irish Quidditch League; every year thirteen teams compete for the League Cup

1883 Goal baskets are replaced with goalposts topped with hoops for fairer play, to the anger of many fans

1652 The first European Cup

1884 A new rule states that only the Chaser carrying the Quaffle can enter the scoring area, to prevent other Chasers from ramming the Keeper aside

1620 The pitch now has scoring areas and Keepers are advised to stay within them

1600s The World Cup becomes truly worldwide, with countries from outside Europe competing

1926 The invention of the Cleansweep One, the first racing broom designed for sporting use

1994 Harry Potter attends the Quidditch World Cup final between Ireland and Bulgaria

1538 Using wands against the opposing team is banned, preventing many magical fouls

3

SPELLBINDING SPACES AND PECULIAR PLACES

Discover the head-spinning ways into and through the wizarding world. Lose yourself in the chitter-chatter of Diagon Alley, and peep into the shops that have been selling magical wares for longer than anyone cares to remember. Take a tour of the Burrow and enjoy a picture postcard view of Hogsmeade in the snow. Complete your journey with a trip to platform nine and three-quarters as the Hogwarts Express gets ready to depart.

HARRY'S CORNER
OF THE WIZARDING WORLD

HOGWARTS
SCHOOL OF WITCHCRAFT
AND WIZARDRY
Magically hidden

HOGSMEADE

SPINNER'S END

SCOTLAND

· THE LOVEGOODS' HOUSE · South Coast ·

NORTHERN
IRELAND

COKEWORTH
Midlands

FOREST OF DEAN
Gloucestershire

UPPER FLAGLEY
Yorkshire

WALES

· GODRIC'S HOLLOW · West Country ·

1994 QUIDDITCH
WORLD CUP STADIUM
Dartmoor, Devon

ENGLAND

LONDON

SHELL COTTAGE
Tinworth, Cornwall

THE BURROW

OTTERY ST.
CATCHPOLE
South Coast

LITTLE WHINGING
Surrey

AZKABAN
Unplottable

PLATFORM NINE AND THREE-QUARTERS
King's Cross Station

THE LEAKY CAULDRON
Charing Cross Road

DIAGON ALLEY

NUMBER TWELVE, GRIMMAULD PLACE
Unplottable

THE MINISTRY OF MAGIC

ST. MUNGO'S HOSPITAL
FOR MAGICAL MALADIES AND INJURIES

NUMBER FOUR, PRIVET DRIVE

◦ LITTLE HANGLETON ◦

S
67

◦ MALFOY MANOR ◦ Wiltshire ◦

WELCOME TO DIAGON ALLEY

"NO, CROOKSHANKS, NO!"

"You *bought* that monster?"

"Mum, can I have a Pygmy Puff?"

"He's *gorgeous*, isn't he?"

"Dragon liver, sixteen Sickles an ounce, they're mad. . . ."

"'Can we buy all this in London?' Harry wondered aloud. 'If yeh know where to go,' said Hagrid.**"**

How to enter Diagon Alley, the famous wizarding shopping street

1. Go into the Leaky Cauldron on Charing Cross Road (it's the shabby pub Muggles can't see)

2. Find the small, walled courtyard (go through the bar and out the back door)

3. Count the bricks above the dustbin (three up . . . two across . . .)

4. Tap the wall three times

"What about those *Monster Books*, eh? The assistant nearly cried when we said we wanted two."

"*Unfogging the Future.* Very good guide to all your basic fortune-telling methods — palmistry, crystal balls, bird entrails —"

"*A study of Hogwarts Prefects and their later careers.* . . . That sounds fascinating . . . ."

"Look . . . the new Nimbus Two Thousand — fastest ever —"

"The usual, Hagrid?"

"The brick he had touched quivered — it wriggled — in the middle, a small hole appeared — it grew wider and wider — a second later they were facing an archway large enough even for Hagrid, an archway onto a cobbled street that twisted and turned out of sight.**"**

"It's a lunascope, old boy — no more messing around with moon charts, see?"

"Well, if you don't want a replacement, you can try this rat tonic."

"*Famous Harry Potter.* . . . Can't even go into a *bookshop* without making the front page."

"Try this one. Beechwood and dragon heartstring. Nine inches. Nice and flexible. Just take it and give it a wave."

"That's three Galleons, nine Sickles, and a Knut. . . . Cough up."

"Just come out— prototype —"

"Oh, I wouldn't read that if I were you. . . . You'll start seeing death omens everywhere. It's enough to frighten anyone to death."

"I remember every wand I've ever sold, Mr. Potter. Every single wand."

"I'm never stocking them again, never! It's been bedlam! I thought we'd seen the worst when we bought two hundred copies of *The Invisible Book of Invisibility* — cost a fortune, and we never found them. . . ."

"Listen, Harry, would yeh mind if I slipped off fer a pick-me-up in the Leaky Cauldron? I hate them Gringotts carts."

"I think we must expect great things from you, Mr. Potter . . . ."

"It's the fastest broom in the world, isn't it, Dad?"

"My father's next door buying my books and Mother's up the street looking at wands."

"I think I'll bully Father into getting me one and I'll smuggle it in somehow."

"Irish International Side's just put in an order for seven of these beauties!"

NUMBER ONE, DIAGON ALLEY

The oldest pub in London, it has stood in this spot since before Charing Cross Road existed

It's said that it was built at the same time as Diagon Alley, in the early sixteenth century

One of the Leaky Cauldron's beers, Gamp's Old Gregarious, tastes so awful that no one has ever managed to finish a pint

There are several bedrooms upstairs for travelers

When Harry stays in room eleven, it has a comfortable bed, polished oak furniture, a fire, and a talking mirror over the basin

"Harry could hear the buses rolling by in the unseen Muggle street behind him and the sound of the invisible crowd below in Diagon Alley."

THE SHOPS OF DIAGON — ALLEY —

LEAKY CAULDRON 1

GAMBOL AND JAPES WIZARDING JOKE SHOP 4

5 **FLOREAN FORTESCUE'S ICE-CREAM PARLOUR**

6

7

ALL SIZES
COPPER, BRASS
PEWTER, SILVER
SELF-STIRRING
COLLAPSIBLE
CAULDRONS

OBSCURUS BOOKS 3

Gringotts WIZARDING BANK

Madam Malkin's ROBES FOR ALL OCCASIONS 2

" There were shops selling robes, shops selling telescopes and strange silver instruments Harry had never seen before, windows stacked with barrels of bat spleens and eels' eyes, tottering piles of spell books, quills and rolls of parchment, potion bottles, globes of the moon . . . . "

THE APOTHECARY
· DIAGON ALLEY ·

POWDERED HORN *of a* BICORN

"Then they visited the Apothecary, which was fascinating enough to make up for its horrible smell, a mixture of bad eggs and rotted cabbages. Barrels of slimy stuff stood on the floor; jars of herbs, dried roots, and bright powders lined the walls; bundles of feathers, strings of fangs, and snarled claws hung from the ceiling."

FLUXWEED

S 74

FLOBBERWORMS

Mucus used to thicken potions

Powdered Root of Asphodel

Add to infusion of wormwood for the Draught of Living Death

BEZOARS

A stone from a goat's stomach, antidote to most poisons

BOOMSLANG SKIN

THYME

USEFUL FOR A SHRINKING SOLUTION:

- Daisy roots (chopped)
- Shrivelfig (skinned)
- Caterpillar (sliced)
- Rat spleen (only one)
- Leech juice (just a dash)

RAT SPLEENS

GILLYWEED
For breathing underwater

PICKLED MURTLAP
+ TENTACLES +

Essence of Murtlap soothes bleeding and boils; when eaten, its growths promote resistance to curses and jinxes

Overdose may cause unsightly purple ear hair

Find a recipe for the Draught of Living Death on page 145 ➤

DRAGON CLAWS

Reportedly good for brain boosts when powdered

DRAGON LIVER

16 SICKLES AN OUNCE

BEETLE EYES

5 KNUTS A SCOOP

EEL EYES

SNAKE FANGS

SIMPLE POTION TO CURE BOILS:

- Crushed snake fangs
- Dried nettles

Leeches

WOLFSBANE

Also known as aconite or monkshood

ESSENCE OF DITTANY

For wounds

Used in love potions
May be eaten whole as a cure for ague

FROZEN ASHWINDER EGGS

INFUSION of WORMWOOD

S
75

VALERIAN ROOT

POLYJUICE POTION CONTAINS:

- Lacewing flies (stewed for 21 days)
- Leeches
- Fluxweed (picked at the full moon)
- Knotgrass
- Horn of a Bicorn (powdered)
- Boomslang skin (shredded)
- A bit of whoever you want to change into

LACEWING FLIES

Fobberknoll Feathers

Used in Truth Serums and Memory Potions

UNICORN HORN

SOPOPHOROUS BEANS

POWDERED MOONSTONE

Mixed with syrup of hellebore in the Draught of Peace

KNOTGRASS

21 GALLEONS

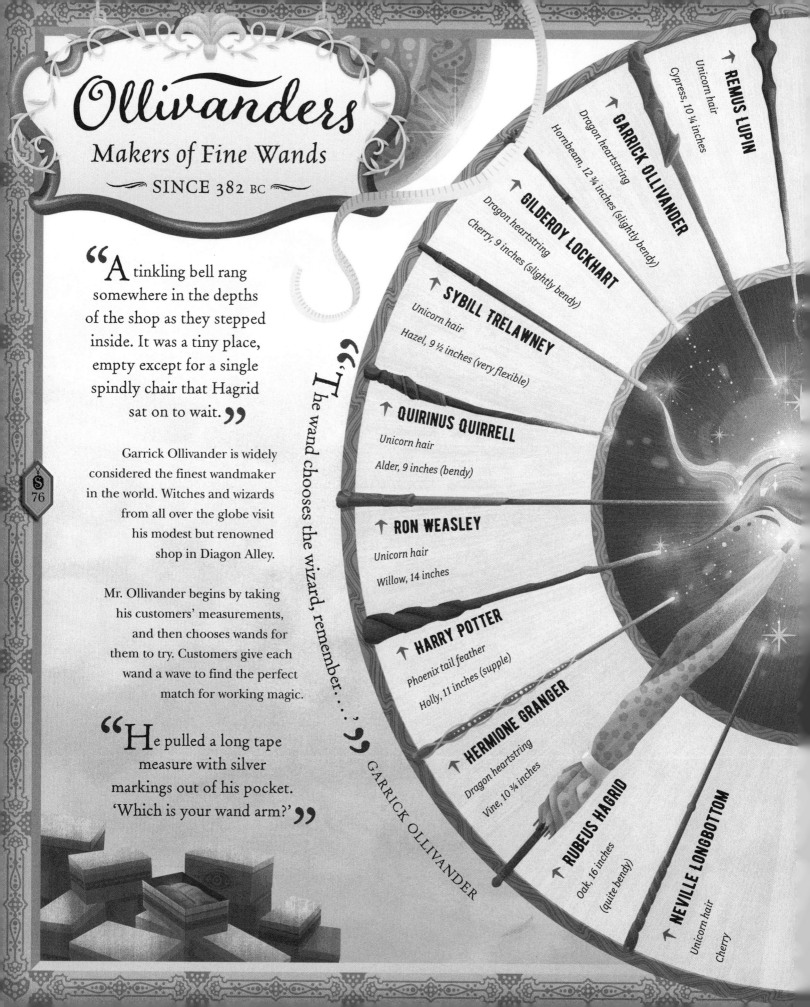

Ollivanders
Makers of Fine Wands
— SINCE 382 BC —

"A tinkling bell rang somewhere in the depths of the shop as they stepped inside. It was a tiny place, empty except for a single spindly chair that Hagrid sat on to wait."

Garrick Ollivander is widely considered the finest wandmaker in the world. Witches and wizards from all over the globe visit his modest but renowned shop in Diagon Alley.

Mr. Ollivander begins by taking his customers' measurements, and then chooses wands for them to try. Customers give each wand a wave to find the perfect match for working magic.

"He pulled a long tape measure with silver markings out of his pocket. 'Which is your wand arm?'"

"The wand chooses the wizard, remember..."
GARRICK OLLIVANDER

↑ REMUS LUPIN
Unicorn hair
Cypress, 10 ¾ inches

↑ GARRICK OLLIVANDER
Dragon heartstring
Hornbeam, 12 ¾ inches (slightly bendy)

↑ GILDEROY LOCKHART
Dragon heartstring
Cherry, 9 inches (slightly bendy)

↑ SYBILL TRELAWNEY
Unicorn hair
Hazel, 9 ½ inches (very flexible)

↑ QUIRINUS QUIRRELL
Unicorn hair
Alder, 9 inches (bendy)

↑ RON WEASLEY
Unicorn hair
Willow, 14 inches

↑ HARRY POTTER
Phoenix tail feather
Holly, 11 inches (supple)

↑ HERMIONE GRANGER
Dragon heartstring
Vine, 10 ¾ inches

↑ RUBEUS HAGRID
Oak, 16 inches (quite bendy)

↑ NEVILLE LONGBOTTOM
Unicorn hair
Cherry

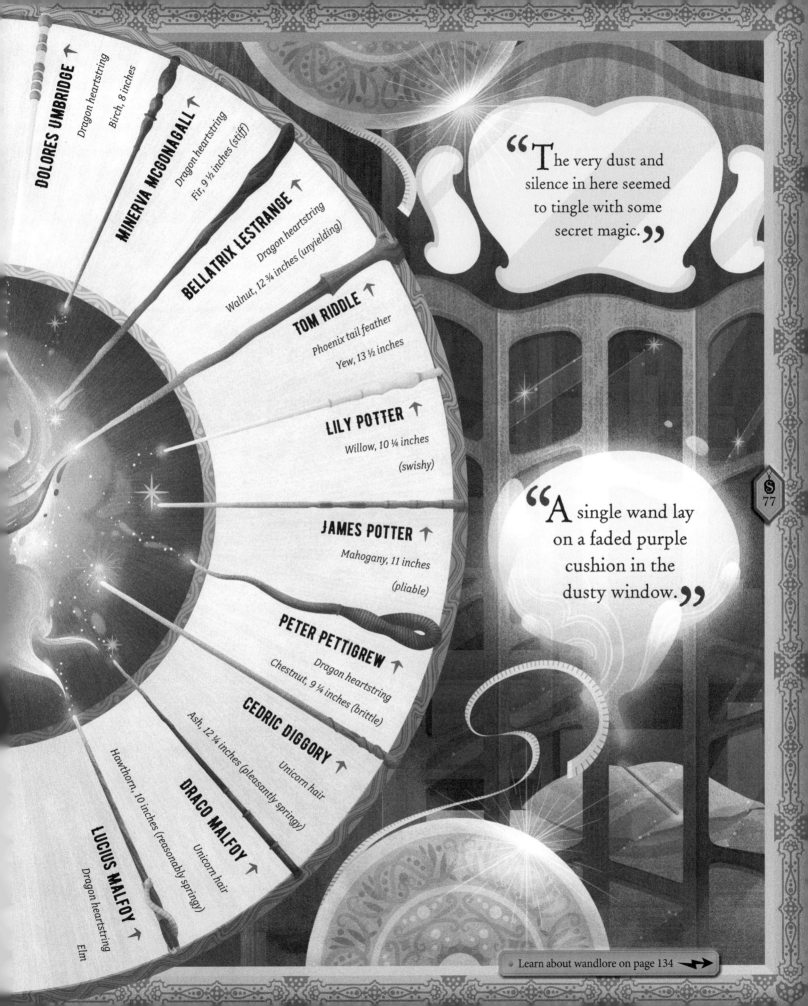

DOLORES UMBRIDGE ↑

Dragon heartstring

Birch, 8 inches

MINERVA MCGONAGALL ↑

Dragon heartstring

Fir, 9½ inches (stiff)

BELLATRIX LESTRANGE ↑

Dragon heartstring

Walnut, 12¾ inches (unyielding)

TOM RIDDLE ↑

Phoenix tail feather

Yew, 13½ inches

LILY POTTER ↑

Willow, 10¼ inches

(swishy)

JAMES POTTER ↑

Mahogany, 11 inches

(pliable)

PETER PETTIGREW ↑

Dragon heartstring

Chestnut, 9¼ inches (brittle)

CEDRIC DIGGORY ↑

Unicorn hair

Ash, 12¼ inches (pleasantly springy)

DRACO MALFOY ↑

Unicorn hair

Hawthorn, 10 inches (reasonably springy)

LUCIUS MALFOY ↑

Dragon heartstring

Elm

> "The very dust and silence in here seemed to tingle with some secret magic."

> "A single wand lay on a faded purple cushion in the dusty window."

Learn about wandlore on page 134 ➜

NO. 93 DIAGON ALLEY
WEASLEYS' WIZARD WHEEZES

"Fred and George's windows hit the eye like a firework display. Casual passersby were looking back over their shoulders at the windows, and a few rather stunned-looking people had actually come to a halt, transfixed. The left-hand window was dazzlingly full of an assortment of goods that revolved, popped, flashed, bounced, and shrieked."

DAYDREAM CHARMS

PATENTED DAYDREAM CHARMS
EASY TO FIT INTO THE AVERAGE SCHOOL LESSON
AND VIRTUALLY UNDETECTABLE
(SIDE-EFFECTS INCLUDE VACANT EXPRESSION AND MINOR DROOLING)

✷ NOT FOR SALE TO UNDER-SIXTEENS ✷

PYGMY PUFFS

"'If anyone fancies buying a Portable Swamp, as demonstrated upstairs, come to number ninety-three, Diagon Alley — Weasleys' Wizard Wheezes . . . Our new premises!'"

FRED WEASLEY

SHIELD GLOVES & HATS

Hats bought by the Ministry of Magic for its support staff

SHIELD CLOAKS

EDIBLE DARK MARKS
THEY'LL MAKE ANYONE SICK!

TON-TONGUE TOFFEE

BLOOD BLISTERPODS

Canary Creams
7 Sickles each

EXTENDABLE EARS

OWL ORDER SERVICE

ALSO DISGUISES PRODUCTS SO THEY WON'T BE CONFISCATED

SKIVING SNACKBOXES
• PUKING PASTILLES •
• FEVER FUDGE •
• FAINTING FANCIES •
• NOSEBLEED NOUGAT •

Secret ingredients: Doxy venom, Venomous Tentacula seeds, Murtlap essence

DOUBLE-ENDED, COLOR-CODED CHEWS

~~TASTED AND TESTED~~ BANNED AT HOGWARTS

EAT ONE HALF TO GET OUT OF YOUR LESSON,

THEN EAT THE OTHER HALF TO RETURN TO FULL FITNESS AND AVOID UNPROFITABLE BOREDOM

FAINTING FANCIES

NOSEBLEED NOUGAT

PUKING PASTILLES

FEVER FUDGE

PUKING PASTILLES

FAINTING FANCIES

WEASLEYS' WILDFIRE WHIZ-BANGS

BASIC BLAZE – 5 GALLEONS
DEFLAGRATION DELUXE – 20 GALLEONS

WEASLEYS' WIZARD WHEEZES

NO. 93

ALL joke items are under a BLANKET BAN at Hogwarts

HEADLESS
2 GALLEONS EACH
HATS

WHY ARE YOU WORRYING
about
YOU-KNOW-WHO?
You **SHOULD** *be worrying about*
U-NO-POO
☞ THE CONSTIPATION ☜
SENSATION
That's GRIPPING *the Nation!*

WONDERWITCH

LOVE POTIONS
Will work for up to twenty-four hours

GUARANTEED
Ten-Second Pimple Vanisher

TRICK WANDS

DECOY DETONATORS

"And our Decoy Detonators are just walking off the shelves, look." FRED WEASLEY

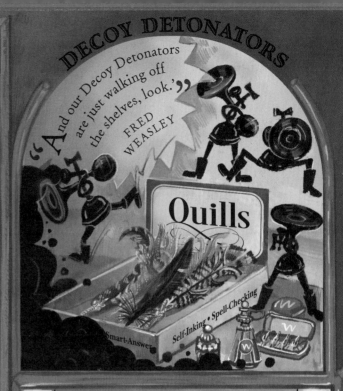

Quills
Smart-Answer · Self-Inking · Spell-Checking

MUGGLE MAGIC TRICKS

S 79

INSTANT DARKNESS POWDER

"Look, Instant Darkness Powder, we're importing it from Peru. Handy if you want to make a quick escape." GEORGE WEASLEY

Joke Cauldrons

TRICK WANDS

WELCOME

NUMBER TWELVE, GRIMMAULD PLACE

Number twelve, Grimmauld Place is the ancestral home of the Black family — one of the oldest wizarding families.

Sirius's teenage bedroom

GRYFFINDOR

"Harry thought, and no sooner had he reached the part about number twelve, Grimmauld Place, than a battered door emerged out of nowhere between numbers eleven and thirteen, followed swiftly by dirty walls and grimy windows. It was as though an extra house had inflated, pushing those on either side out of its way. Harry gaped at it. The stereo in number eleven thudded on. Apparently the Muggles inside hadn't felt anything."

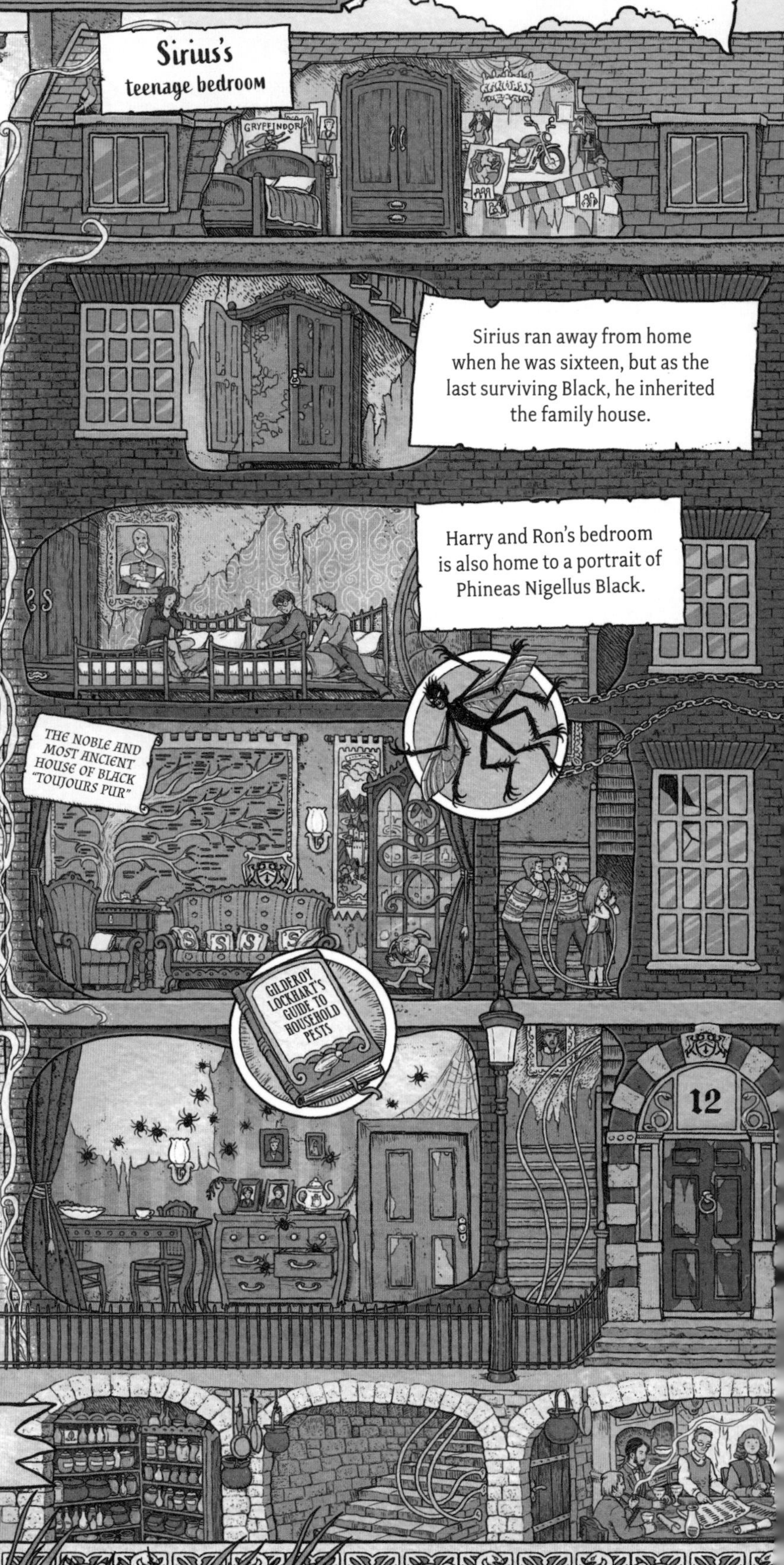

Sirius ran away from home when he was sixteen, but as the last surviving Black, he inherited the family house.

Harry and Ron's bedroom is also home to a portrait of Phineas Nigellus Black.

THE NOBLE AND MOST ANCIENT HOUSE OF BLACK "TOUJOURS PUR"

GILDEROY LOCKHART'S GUIDE TO HOUSEHOLD PESTS

11

12

It is about a twenty-minute walk from Grimmauld Place to King's Cross station.

'Hasn't anyone told you? This was my parents' house,' said Sirius. 'But I'm the last Black left, so it's mine now. I offered it to Dumbledore for headquarters — about the only useful thing I've been able to do.'

Regulus's teenage bedroom

Do Not Enter Without the Express Permission of Regulus Arcturus Black

Buckbeak lives in Mrs. Black's bedroom.

'It's ideal for headquarters, of course,' Sirius said. 'My father put every security measure known to wizard-kind on it when he lived here. It's Unplottable, so Muggles could never come and call — as if they'd have wanted to — and now Dumbledore's added his protection, you'd be hard put to find a safer house anywhere.'

The house is unplottable and hidden from sight by a powerful Fidelius Charm.

Mrs. Black's portrait and the Black family tree seem to be stuck to the walls with a Permanent Sticking Charm.

13

Kreacher's cupboard

Number twelve, Grimmauld Place is home to Kreacher the house-elf, who had lived there alone for ten years before the Order of the Phoenix moved in. He sleeps under a boiler in a cupboard off the kitchen, where he keeps his most treasured possessions.

• See Phineas Nigellus Black's portrait at Hogwarts on page 111 ➡➡

The Burrow

The Burrow is home to the Weasley family, and can be found a little way outside the Muggle village of Ottery St. Catchpole.

"The Weasleys' house burst with the strange and unexpected. Harry got a shock the first time he looked in the mirror over the kitchen mantelpiece and it shouted, *'Tuck your shirt in, scruffy!'* The ghoul in the attic howled and dropped pipes whenever he felt things were getting too quiet, and small explosions from Fred and George's bedroom were considered perfectly normal. What Harry found most unusual about life at Ron's, however, wasn't the talking mirror or the clanking ghoul: It was the fact that everybody there seemed to like him."

"Harry, grinning widely, said, 'This is the best house I've ever been in.' Ron's ears went pink."

Harry thinks of the Burrow as his "second favorite building in the world."

The Kitchen

"Ron was in there . . . and so was Mrs. Weasley, who could cook better than anyone he knew. . . ."

The BURROW

The Ghoul in the Attic

Ron's Bedroom

Fred and George's Bedroom

The Weasley Family Clock

MORTAL PERIL

PRISON

HOME

HOSPITAL

SCHOOL

LOST

WORK

TRAVELING

MOLLY · GINNY · FRED · GEORGE · RON · PERCY · ARTHUR · CHARLIE · BILL

The Weasleys own an adjacent field surrounded by trees, where they can play Quidditch unseen by local Muggles.

The Weasleys' garage is also a workshop where Mr. Weasley can tinker with his collection of Muggle gadgets.

The garden needs to be regularly de-gnomed.

Hogsmeade is a wizarding village, and the only entirely non-Muggle settlement in Britain.

It was founded by Hengist of Woodcroft about a thousand years ago, around the same time as Hogwarts.

Hogsmeade was the headquarters for the 1612 goblin rebellion.

Hogwarts students in their third year and above may visit the village on certain weekends, but they need a permission slip signed by a parent or guardian.

HOGSMEADE VILLAGE

S 84

HONEYDUKES SWEETSHOP

ZONKO'S JOKE SHOP

"Hogsmeade looked like a Christmas card . . . shops were all covered in a layer of crisp snow; there were holly wreaths on the doors and strings of enchanted candles hanging in the trees."

Hogsmeade is home to the Shrieking Shack, said to be the most severely haunted building in Britain.

The Marauder's Map shows secret passages that lead from the Whomping Willow to the Shrieking Shack, and from the statue of the one-eyed witch to the cellar of Honeydukes Sweetshop.

Hogsmeade station is set a little way apart from the village.

Can you find all seven passages to Hogsmeade on page 118?

GLADRAGS WIZARDWEAR

LONDON ~ PARIS ~ HOGSMEADE

"They went into Gladrags Wizardwear to buy a present for Dobby, where they had fun selecting all the most lurid socks they could find, including a pair patterned with flashing gold and silver stars, and another that screamed loudly when they became too smelly."

THE HOG'S HEAD

"We're not out of bounds; I specifically asked Professor Flitwick whether students were allowed to come in the Hog's Head, and he said yes, but he advised me strongly to bring our own glasses.'"

HERMIONE GRANGER

THE POST OFFICE

"The owls sat hooting softly down at him, at least three hundred of them; from Great Grays right down to tiny little Scops owls ("Local Deliveries Only")."

For more on communication, see page 42

For more on owls, see page 44

Scrivenshaft's QUILL SHOP

THREE BROOMSTICKS

Madam **Puddifoot's**

DERVISH AND BANGES
Wizarding Equipment

(S) 85

HONEYDUKES SWEETSHOP

"SPECIAL EFFECTS" SWEETS

Drooble's Best Blowing Gum

Toothflossing Stringmints

Pepper Imps

Ice Mice

Peppermint Toads

Sugar Quills

Exploding Bonbons

ZONKO'S JOKE SHOP

"They left Zonko's with their money bags considerably lighter than they had been on entering, but their pockets bulging with Dungbombs, Hiccup Sweets, Frog Spawn Soap, and a Nose-Biting Teacup apiece."

THE SHRIEKING SHACK

"Even the Hogwarts ghosts avoid it,' said Ron as they leaned on the fence, looking up at it. 'I asked Nearly Headless Nick . . . he says he's heard a very rough crowd lives here. No one can get in. Fred and George tried, obviously, but all the entrances are sealed shut. . . .'"

Discover even more wizarding treats on page 53

PLATFORM NINE
AND THREE-QUARTERS

To travel to Hogwarts School of Witchcraft and Wizardry at the start of the school year, students must board the famous Hogwarts Express. It departs on the first of September from London King's Cross station, platform nine and three-quarters, at eleven o'clock precisely.

Platform nine and three-quarters can be found by walking straight through the apparently solid barrier dividing platforms nine and ten.

The tricky part is doing this without attracting the attention of any Muggles.

★★KING'S CROSS★★
★SEPTEMBER 1ST★
HOGWARTS EXPRESS
PLATFORM 9¾
9¾

"A scarlet steam engine was waiting next to a platform packed with people. A sign overhead said *Hogwarts Express, eleven o'clock*. Harry looked behind him and saw a wrought-iron archway where the ticket barrier had been, with the words *Platform Nine and Three-Quarters* on it. He had done it."

Where exactly the Hogwarts Express came from is unknown, although there are records at the Ministry of Magic detailing the performance of one hundred and sixty-seven Memory Charms and the largest ever mass Concealment Charm cast in Britain. The morning after these alleged crimes, the arrival of a scarlet steam engine astounded the villagers of Hogsmeade, while Muggle railway workers in Crewe were left with the uncomfortable feeling that they had mislaid something very important.

The train has a trolley which passes through the carriages at one o'clock. Treats include Bertie Bott's Every Flavor Beans, Drooble's Best Blowing Gum, Chocolate Frogs, Pumpkin Pasties, Cauldron Cakes, and Licorice Wands.

"The countryside now flying past the window was becoming wilder. The neat fields had gone. Now there were woods, twisting rivers, and dark green hills."

School Prefects travel in their own carriage and patrol the corridors from time to time.

Students must change into their school robes before the train reaches Hogsmeade station.

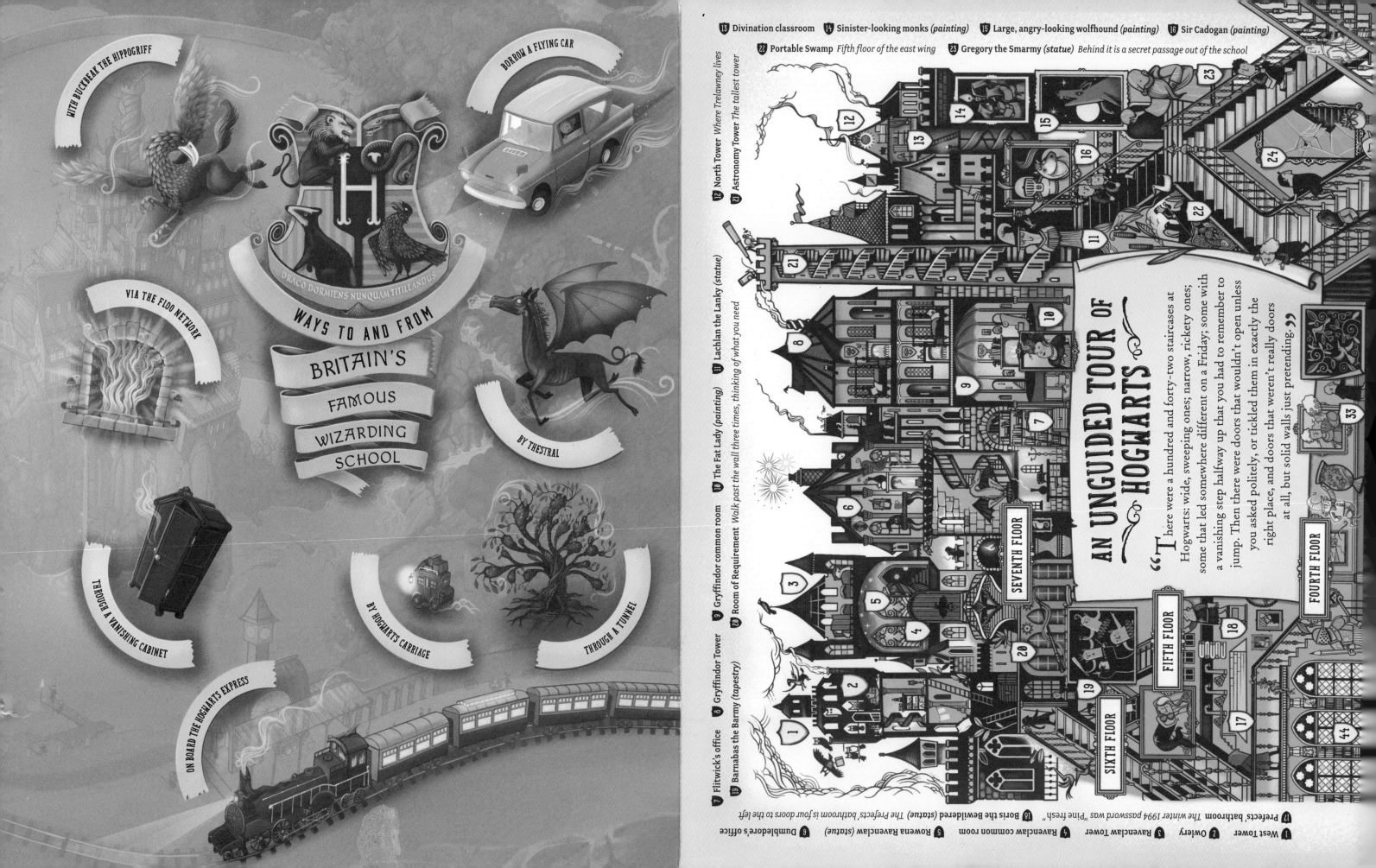

WITH BUCKBEAK THE HIPPOGRIFF

BORROW A FLYING CAR

VIA THE FLOO NETWORK

WAYS TO AND FROM

Draco Dormiens Nunquam Titillandus

BRITAIN'S FAMOUS WIZARDING SCHOOL

BY THESTRAL

THROUGH A VANISHING CABINET

BY HOGWARTS CARRIAGE

THROUGH A TUNNEL

ON BOARD THE HOGWARTS EXPRESS

---

13 **Divination classroom** 14 **Sinister-looking monks** (*painting*) 15 **Large, angry-looking wolfhound** (*painting*) 16 **Sir Cadogan** (*painting*)

22 **Portable Swamp** *Fifth floor of the east wing* 23 **Gregory the Smarmy** (*statue*) *Behind it is a secret passage out of the school*

12 **North Tower** *Where Trelawney lives* 21 **Astronomy Tower** *The tallest tower* 11 **Lachlan the Lanky** (*statue*) 10 **The Fat Lady** (*painting*) *Walk past the wall three times, thinking of what you need* 9 **Gryffindor common room** 8 **Gryffindor Tower**

7 **Flitwick's office** 19 **Barnabas the Barmy** (*tapestry*)

1 **West Tower** 2 **Owlery** 3 **Ravenclaw Tower** 4 **Ravenclaw common room** 5 **Rowena Ravenclaw** (*statue*) 6 **Dumbledore's office**

17 **Prefects bathroom** *The winter 1994 password was "Pine fresh"* 18 **Boris the Bewildered** (*statue*) *The Prefects' bathroom is four doors to the left*

20 **Room of Requirement**

SEVENTH FLOOR

SIXTH FLOOR

FIFTH FLOOR

FOURTH FLOOR

AN UNGUIDED TOUR OF HOGWARTS

"There were a hundred and forty-two staircases at Hogwarts: wide, sweeping ones; narrow, rickety ones; some that led somewhere different on a Friday; some with a vanishing step halfway up that you had to remember to jump. Then there were doors that wouldn't open unless you asked politely, or tickled them in exactly the right place, and doors that weren't really doors at all, but solid walls just pretending."

ASTRONOMY TOWER

HAGRID'S HUT

WHOMPING WILLOW

GREENHOUSES

HOGWARTS CASTLE

FORBIDDEN FOREST

"The narrow path had opened suddenly onto the edge of a great black lake. Perched atop a high mountain on the other side, its windows sparkling in the starry sky, was a vast castle with many turrets and towers."

SCHOOL WALLS

HOGSMEADE STATION

HOGWARTS EXPRESS

4

AN INVITATION TO HOGWARTS

Every year on the first of September, students go back to Hogwarts. Take an unguided tour of the castle, exploring every nook and cranny. Learn about the Sorting Ceremony, houses and common rooms, as well as professors and their subjects. Look for ghosts in the Great Hall, study Hogwarts library books, and visit the Room of Requirement. You might even discover the secrets of the Marauder's Map. Mischief managed!

CATCH THE KNIGHT BUS

BY BROOMSTICK

WITH FAWKES THE PHOENIX

WELCOME TO
HOGWARTS
SCHOOL OF
WITCHCRAFT
AND
WIZARDRY

DRACO DORMIENS NUNQUAM TITILLANDUS

BY PORTKEY

ABOARD THE BEAUXBATONS

ON BOARD THE DURMSTRANG SHIP

BY BOAT ACROSS THE LAKE

FLYING CARRIAGE

SCHOOL GATES

QUIDDITCH STADIUM

BROOM SHED

PRACTICE PITCH

GREAT LAKE

❝ 'Welcome!' said Dumbledore, the candlelight shimmering on his beard. 'Welcome to another year at Hogwarts!' **❞**

HOGSMEADE

❝ And the fleet of little boats moved off all at once, gliding across the lake, which was as smooth as glass. Everyone was silent, staring up at the great castle overhead. It towered over them as they sailed nearer and nearer to the cliff on which it stood. **❞**

SHRIEKING SHACK

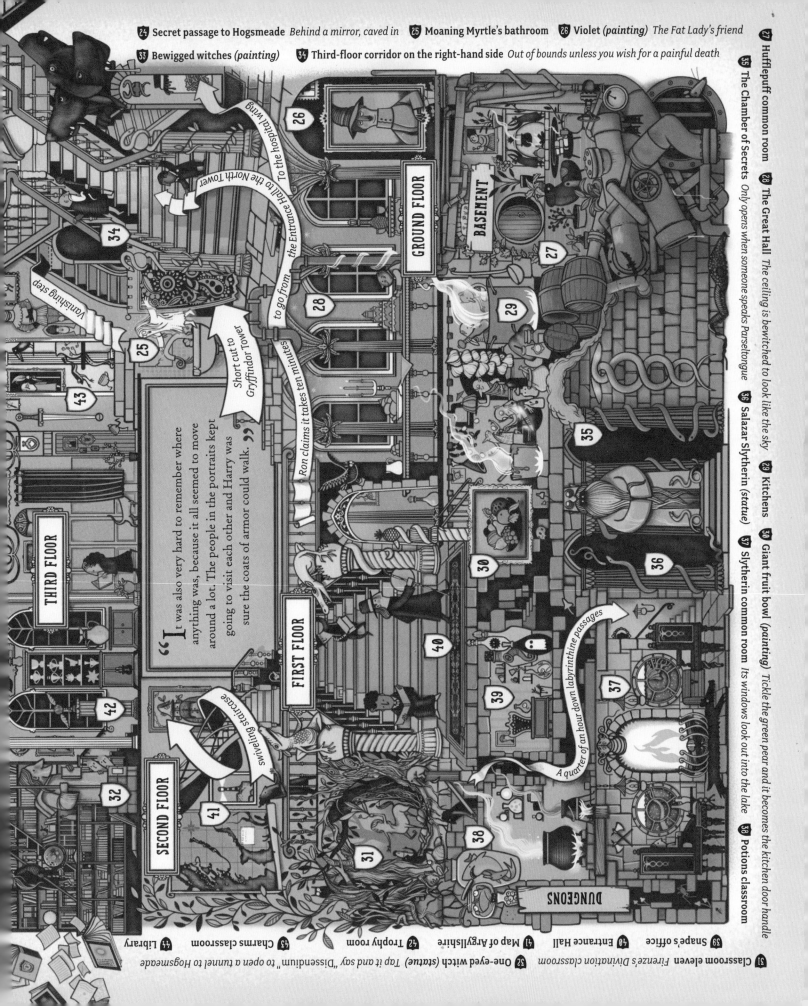

24 Secret passage to Hogsmeade *Behind a mirror, caved in* **25** Moaning Myrtle's bathroom **26** Violet *(painting) The Fat Lady's friend* **27** Hufflepuff common room **28** The Great Hall *The ceiling is bewitched to look like the sky* **29** Kitchens **30** Giant fruit bowl *(painting) Tickle the green pear and it becomes the kitchen door handle*

33 Bewigged witches *(painting)* **34** Third-floor corridor on the right-hand side *Out of bounds unless you wish for a painful death* **35** The Chamber of Secrets *Only opens when someone speaks Parseltongue* **36** Salazar Slytherin *(statue)* **37** Slytherin common room *Its windows look out into the lake* **38** Potions classroom

to go from the Entrance Hall to the hospital wing

To the North Tower

Vanishing step

Short cut to Gryffindor Tower

Ron claims it takes ten minutes

"It was also very hard to remember where anything was, because it all seemed to move around a lot. The people in the portraits kept going to visit each other and Harry was sure the coats of armor could walk."

swiveling staircase

A quarter of an hour down labyrinthine passages

GROUND FLOOR

BASEMENT

THIRD FLOOR

FIRST FLOOR

SECOND FLOOR

DUNGEONS

31 Classroom eleven *Firenze's Divination classroom* **32** One-eyed witch *(statue) Tap it and say "Dissendium" to open a tunnel to Hogsmeade* **39** Snape's office **40** Entrance Hall **41** Map of Argyllshire **42** Trophy room **43** Charms classroom **44** Library

The Sorting Hat

> "Professor McGonagall silently placed a four-legged stool in front of the first years. On top of the stool she put a pointed wizard's hat. This hat was patched and frayed and extremely dirty."

> "'Welcome to Hogwarts,' said Professor McGonagall. 'The start-of-term banquet will begin shortly, but before you take your seats in the Great Hall, you will be sorted into your Houses.'"

- The Sorting Hat places all Hogwarts first-year students into their school Houses

- The Hat can look into the wearer's mind using a type of magic known as Legilimency

- It divines the wearer's capabilities and can even talk to them and take their choice of House into account

- The Hat sometimes decides on a first-year's House instantly and sometimes it takes several minutes

- Students who take more than five minutes to be sorted are called Hatstalls

A HISTORY OF THE HAT

- The story goes that it once belonged to Godric Gryffindor and was bewitched to hold the intelligence of all four founders of Hogwarts

- Every Hogwarts student since the days of the founders has worn the Sorting Hat and been placed in a House

- The Hat sits on a shelf in the headmaster's office, and is brought down once a year to sit upon a stool for the Sorting Ceremony

- The Hat sings a different song every year and if it senses that Hogwarts is facing great danger, it may give the school a warning

- Legend has it that in times of great need, a true Gryffindor may pull the sword of Gryffindor out of the Hat

"A rip near the brim opened wide like a mouth — and the hat began to sing:

> '*Oh, you may not think I'm pretty,*
> *But don't judge on what you see,*
> *I'll eat myself if you can find*
> *A smarter hat than me.*
> *You can keep your bowlers black,*
> *Your top hats sleek and tall,*
> *For I'm the Hogwarts Sorting Hat*
> *And I can cap them all.*'"

"'A thousand years or more ago,
When I was newly sewn,
There lived four wizards of renown,
Whose names are still well known:
Bold Gryffindor, from wild moor,
Fair Ravenclaw, from glen,
Sweet Hufflepuff, from valley broad,
Shrewd Slytherin, from fen.
They shared a wish, a hope, a dream,
They hatched a daring plan
To educate young sorcerers
Thus Hogwarts School began.
Now each of these four founders
Formed their own House, for each
Did value different virtues
In the ones they had to teach.
By Gryffindor, the bravest were
Prized far beyond the rest;
For Ravenclaw, the cleverest
Would always be the best;
For Hufflepuff, hard workers were
Most worthy of admission;
And power-hungry Slytherin
Loved those of great ambition.
While still alive they did divide
Their favorites from the throng,
Yet how to pick the worthy ones
When they were dead and gone?
'Twas Gryffindor who found the way,
He whipped me off his head
The founders put some brains in me
So I could choose instead!
Now slip me snug about your ears,
I've never yet been wrong,
I'll have a look inside your mind
And tell where you belong!'"

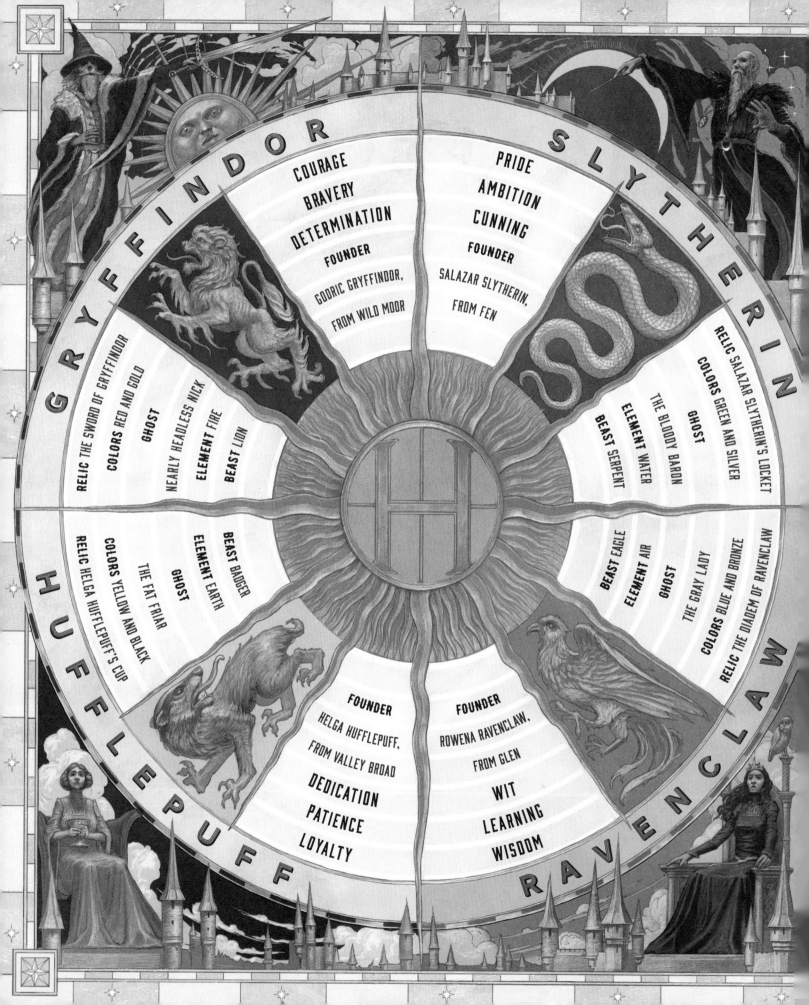

GRYFFINDOR

SLYTHERIN

HUFFLEPUFF

RAVENCLAW

COURAGE
BRAVERY
DETERMINATION
FOUNDER
GODRIC GRYFFINDOR,
FROM WILD MOOR

PRIDE
AMBITION
CUNNING
FOUNDER
SALAZAR SLYTHERIN,
FROM FEN

RELIC THE SWORD OF GRYFFINDOR
COLORS RED AND GOLD
GHOST
NEARLY HEADLESS NICK
ELEMENT FIRE
BEAST LION

RELIC SALAZAR SLYTHERIN'S LOCKET
COLORS GREEN AND SILVER
GHOST
THE BLOODY BARON
ELEMENT WATER
BEAST SERPENT

RELIC HELGA HUFFLEPUFF'S CUP
COLORS YELLOW AND BLACK
GHOST
THE FAT FRIAR
ELEMENT EARTH
BEAST BADGER

RELIC THE DIADEM OF RAVENCLAW
COLORS BLUE AND BRONZE
GHOST
THE GRAY LADY
ELEMENT AIR
BEAST EAGLE

FOUNDER
HELGA HUFFLEPUFF,
FROM VALLEY BROAD
DEDICATION
PATIENCE
LOYALTY

FOUNDER
ROWENA RAVENCLAW,
FROM GLEN
WIT
LEARNING
WISDOM

BROWN, LAVENDER
FINNIGAN, SEAMUS
GRANGER, HERMIONE
LONGBOTTOM, NEVILLE
PATIL, PARVATI
POTTER, HARRY
THOMAS, DEAN
WEASLEY, RONALD

BULSTRODE, MILLICENT
CRABBE, VINCENT
GOYLE, GREGORY
GREENGRASS, DAPHNE
MALFOY, DRACO
NOTT, THEODORE
PARKINSON, PANSY
ZABINI, BLAISE

ABBOTT, HANNAH
BONES, SUSAN
FINCH-FLETCHLEY, JUSTIN
MACMILLAN, ERNIE

BOOT, TERRY
BROCKLEHURST, MANDY
CORNER, MICHAEL
GOLDSTEIN, ANTHONY
PATIL, PADMA
TURPIN, LISA

HARRY'S SORTING CEREMONY

At the start of their first term at Hogwarts,
Harry and his classmates' names are called and
one by one they're sorted into their Houses.

" The Sorting is a very important ceremony because, while you
are here, your House will be something like your family within Hogwarts.
You will have classes with the rest of your House, sleep in your House
dormitory, and spend free time in your House common room.' **"**

PROFESSOR MCGONAGALL

GRYFFINDOR?

" *You might belong in Gryffindor,*
Where dwell the brave at heart,
Their daring, nerve, and chivalry
Set Gryffindors apart.' **"**

HUFFLEPUFF?

" *You might belong in Hufflepuff,*
Where they are just and loyal,
Those patient Hufflepuffs are true
And unafraid of toil.' **"**

SLYTHERIN?

" *Or perhaps in Slytherin*
You'll make your real friends,
Those cunning folk use any means
To achieve their ends.' **"**

RAVENCLAW?

" *Or yet in wise old Ravenclaw,*
If you've a ready mind,
Where those of wit and learning,
Will always find their kind!' **"**

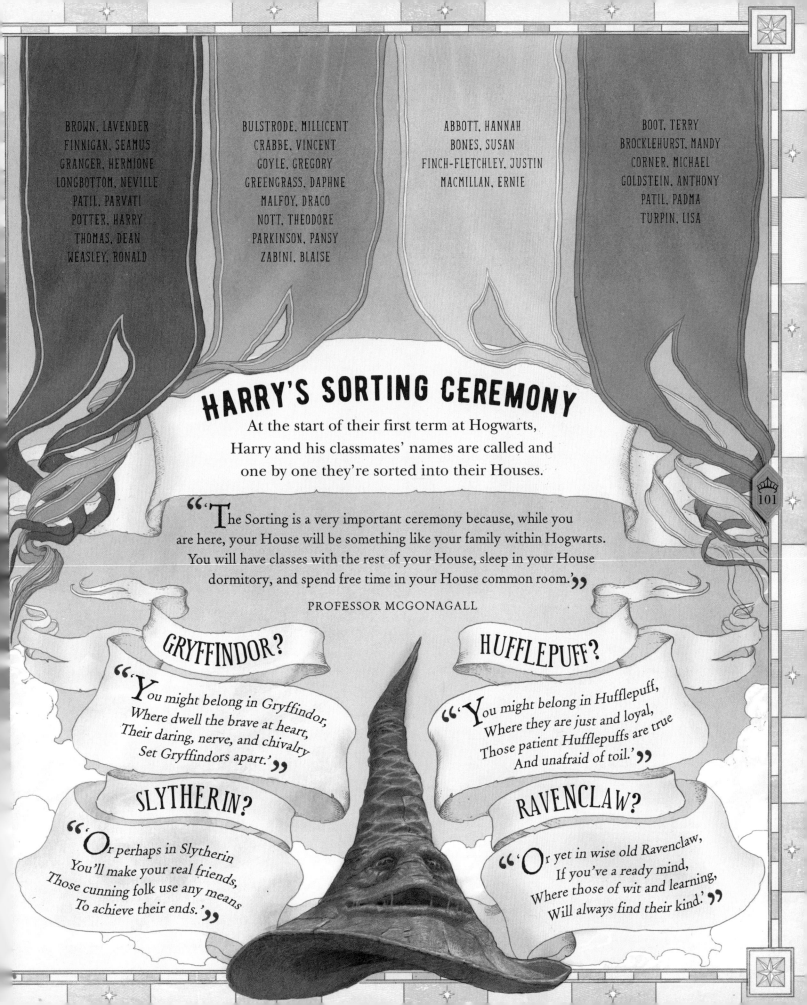

Around the border (clockwise from top): DILLIGROUT • ABSTINENCE • BAUBLES • QUID AGIS • TAPEWORM • MIMBULUS MIMBLETONIA • BANANA FRITTERS • FAIRY LIGHTS • PIG SNOUT • FORTUNA MAJOR • WATTLEBIRD • CAPUT DRACONIS • SCURVY • CUR • ODDSBODIKINS • FLIBBERTIGIBBET • BALDERDASH

NOTABLE MEMBERS

Albus Dumbledore • Sirius Black

ENTRANCE
A circular hole in the wall covered by the Fat Lady's portrait.

HOW TO ENTER
Tell the Fat Lady the password.

Some of the Fat Lady's passwords are in Latin. "*Caput Draconis*" means "dragon's head," "*Fortuna Major*" means "the greater fortune," and "*Quid agis?*" means "how are you?" or "how goes it?"

HEAD OF HOUSE
Professor McGonagall

HOUSE PREFECTS

Hermione Granger • Ron Weasley

COMMON ROOM
In one of the three tallest towers, with an entrance on the seventh floor. From the second floor you can take a short cut through a tapestry.

In a common room full of squashy chairs and rickety tables, the noticeboard has been used for selling old spellbooks, bartering Chocolate Frog Cards. and scouting testers for Fred and George's Skiving Snackboxes.

GRYFFINDOR

"*Said Gryffindor, 'We'll teach all those With brave deeds to their name.'*"

NOTABLE MEMBERS

Tom Riddle ● Horace Slughorn

HOUSE PREFECTS

Draco Malfoy ● Pansy Parkinson

ENTRANCE

A door concealed in a bare, damp stone wall.

HOW TO ENTER

Say the password to the wall.

The Slytherin password changes every fortnight. When Harry and Ron infiltrated the common room on Christmas Day in 1992, the password was *"pure-blood."*

HEAD OF HOUSE

Professor Snape

COMMON ROOM

In the dungeons. You can get there by walking down the stone steps from the Entrance Hall and going deep down labyrinthine passages.

The Slytherin common room is deep under the castle and its windows look out into the lake. Students often see the giant squid swimming past.

⟊ SLYTHERIN ⟊

"*Said Slytherin, 'We'll teach just those Whose ancestry is purest.'*"

104

NOTABLE MEMBERS

Newt Scamander ● Cedric Diggory

HOUSE PREFECTS

Hannah Abbott ● Ernie Macmillan

HEAD OF HOUSE

Professor Sprout

ENTRANCE

Hidden in a stack of barrels, behind the lid in the middle of the second row, two from the bottom.

HOW TO ENTER

Tap the barrel in the rhythm of "Helga Hufflepuff."

If a student taps the wrong rhythm or the wrong barrel to get into the common room, they'll be drenched in vinegar.

COMMON ROOM

In the basement. After going downstairs from the Entrance Hall, walk past the kitchens along a brightly lit corridor decorated with paintings of food.

Professor Sprout, Herbology teacher and Head of Hufflepuff, decorates the common room with all sorts of plants. Some of them talk and dance!

⚜ HUFFLEPUFF ⚜

"Said Hufflepuff, 'I'll teach the lot, And treat them just the same.'"

OR THE FLAME? • A CIRCLE HAS NO BEGINNING • WHERE DO VANISHED OBJECTS GO? • INTO NON-BEING,

WHICH CAME FIRST, THE PHOENIX

WHICH IS TO SAY, EVERYTHING

105

NOTABLE MEMBERS

Garrick Ollivander • Gilderoy Lockhart

HOUSE PREFECTS

Anthony Goldstein • Padma Patil

HEAD OF HOUSE

Professor Flitwick

ENTRANCE

An aged wooden door with a bronze knocker in the shape of an eagle.

HOW TO ENTER

Knock on the door, then answer the question the eagle asks.

Ravenclaws are asked questions instead of being given passwords, to aid their learning. Professor McGonagall, Head of Gryffindor, has been able to enter by answering the question.

COMMON ROOM

In a tall tower on the west side of the castle. A tightly spiraling staircase will take you up to the entrance.

Ravenclaw students believe they have the best views of the school grounds. Through the arched windows they can see the lake and Forbidden Forest, and the mountains beyond.

RAVENCLAW

"Said Ravenclaw, 'We'll teach those whose Intelligence is surest.'"

By the time Halloween arrived, Harry was regretting his rash promise to go to the deathday party. The rest of the school was happily anticipating their Halloween feast; the Great Hall had been decorated with the usual live bats, Hagrid's vast pumpkins had been carved into lanterns large enough for three men to sit in, and there were rumors that Dumbledore had booked a troupe of dancing skeletons for the entertainment.

HOGWARTS AT HALLOWEEN

A thousand live bats fluttered from the walls and ceiling while a thousand more swooped over the tables in low black clouds, making the candles in the pumpkins stutter.

HIGH TABLE

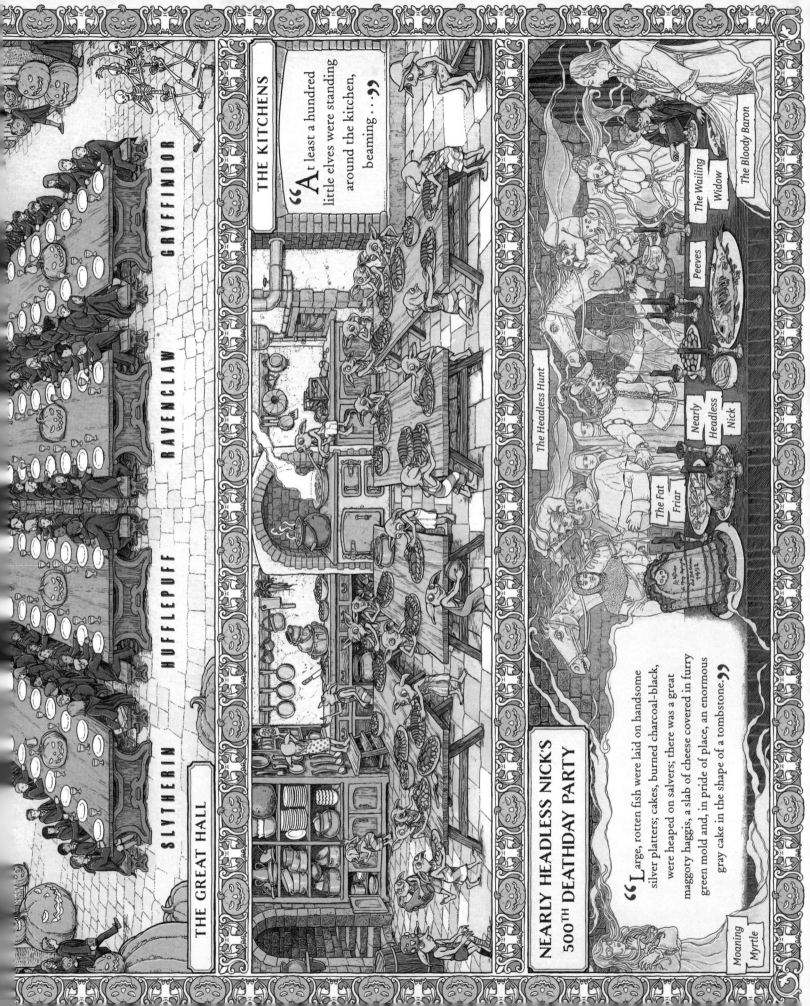

THE GREAT HALL

SLYTHERIN — HUFFLEPUFF — RAVENCLAW — GRYFFINDOR

THE KITCHENS

"At least a hundred little elves were standing around the kitchen, beaming . . ."

NEARLY HEADLESS NICK'S 500TH DEATHDAY PARTY

"Large, rotten fish were laid on handsome silver platters; cakes, burned charcoal-black, were heaped on salvers; there was a great maggoty haggis, a slab of cheese covered in furry green mold and, in pride of place, an enormous gray cake in the shape of a tombstone."

The Headless Hunt

The Fat Friar

Nearly Headless Nick

Peeves

The Wailing Widow

The Bloody Baron

Moaning Myrtle

THE FAT FRIAR

Hufflepuff House is haunted by the Fat Friar.

He was a cheerful monk who was executed because of his suspicious ability to cure the pox by poking patients with a stick.

THE BLOODY BARON

A gaunt and silent specter covered in silver bloodstains.

He is the only ghost at Hogwarts who can really control Peeves.

He wears chains as an act of penitence for crimes he committed in his lifetime.

THE GHOSTS of HOGWARTS

108

"He gasped. So did the people around him. About twenty ghosts had just streamed through the back wall. Pearly-white and slightly transparent, they glided across the room talking to each other and hardly glancing at the first years. They seemed to be arguing."

Hogwarts teaches that a ghost is the imprint of a departed soul left upon the earth.

The Headless Hunt are a ghostly group of huntsmen whose heads have parted company with their bodies.

NEARLY HEADLESS NICK

Nick's full name is Sir Nicholas de Mimsy-Porpington.

Nearly Headless Nick is Gryffindor's House ghost. In life he was a member of the royal court of Henry VII, but was sentenced to death after he tried to straighten the teeth of Lady Grieve and accidentally gave her tusks.

THE HEADLESS HUNT

"Half an inch of skin and sinew holding my neck on, Harry! Most people would think that's good and beheaded, but oh no, it's not enough for Sir Properly Decapitated-Podmore.'"

Nick died on October 31, 1492 by a bungled beheading that took forty-five attempts with a blunt axe.

They enjoy a good game of Horseback Head-Juggling or Head Polo and are led by Sir Patrick Delaney-Podmore.

The most reclusive of the ghosts is the Gray Lady, Ravenclaw's House ghost.

THE GRAY LADY

She was stabbed in a fit of rage by her spurned lover.

Professor Binns is the only ghost teacher at Hogwarts; he teaches History of Magic.

PROFESSOR BINNS

Notoriously, the only exciting part of his class is his habit of entering and leaving through the blackboard.

" '— and then, of course, she went to the Ministry of Magic to stop me stalking her, so I had to come back here and live in my toilet.' "

Myrtle Elizabeth Warren was a student at Hogwarts when she died.

Unlike the other spirits, Peeves is not transparent; instead he can make himself invisible.

"Many people said he hadn't noticed he was dead. He had simply got up to teach one day and left his body behind him in an armchair in front of the staff-room fire; his routine had not varied in the slightest since. "

109

MOANING MYRTLE

She returned after her death to haunt fellow student Olive Hornby.

PEEVES THE POLTERGEIST

The most disastrous attempt to remove Peeves from Hogwarts was made in 1876 by caretaker Rancorous Carpe. It involved an elaborate trap, baited with an assortment of weapons. Not only did Peeves easily escape the trap, he then also had cutlasses, crossbows, a blunderbuss, and a miniature cannon. The castle was evacuated while Peeves amused himself by firing out of the windows and threatening all and sundry with death. A three-day standoff ended with Peeves being allowed additional privileges, such as a once-weekly swim in the boys' toilets on the ground floor, first refusal on stale bread from the kitchen for throwing purposes, and a new hat — to be custom-made by Madame Bonhabille of Paris.

Myrtle is often found haunting one of the girls' bathrooms in Hogwarts, a place with hidden secrets.

Peeves can also move physical objects, making him an airborne menace who loves to cause havoc and distress.

A poltergeist is an entity that can become invisible, slam doors, and create disturbances.

Life cycle of a phoenix

TOFFEE ECLAIRS

ACID POPS

FIZZING WHIZBEE

COCKROACH CLUSTER

LEMON DROP

"Fawkes is a phoenix, Harry. Phoenixes burst into flame when it is time for them to die and are reborn from the ashes. Watch him . . .'"

PROFESSOR DUMBLEDORE

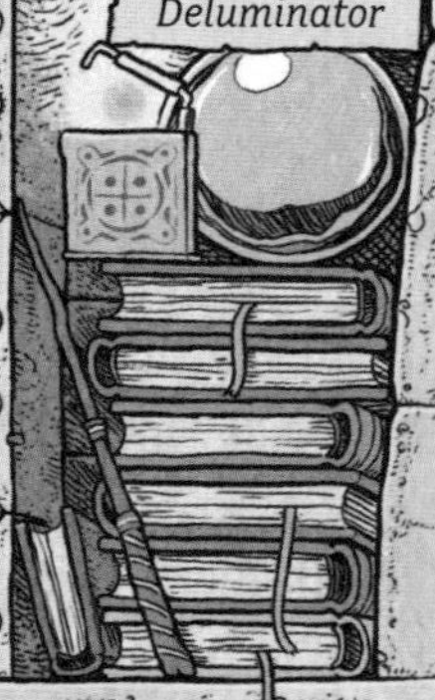

"They rose upward in circles, higher and higher, until at last, slightly dizzy, Harry saw a gleaming oak door ahead, with a brass knocker in the shape of a griffin. He knew now where he was being taken. This must be where Dumbledore lived."

DUMBLEDORE'S OFFICE

"It was a large and beautiful circular room, full of funny little noises. A number of curious silver instruments stood on spindle-legged tables, whirring and emitting little puffs of smoke."

The Deluminator

"The gargoyle sprang suddenly to life and hopped aside as the wall behind him split in two. . . . Behind the wall was a spiral staircase that was moving smoothly upward, like an escalator."

ALBUS DUMBLEDORE

SECRETS OF THE DARKEST ART

HOGWARTS: A History

QUIBBLER

66 A shallow stone basin lay there, with odd carvings around the edge: runes and symbols that Harry did not recognize. The silvery light was coming from the basin's contents, which were like nothing Harry had ever seen before. **99**

The Pensieve

PROFESSOR PHINEAS NIGELLUS BLACK

PROFESSOR ARMANDO DIPPET

DAILY PROPHET

LEMON DROPS

PROFESSOR EVERARD

PROFESSOR DILYS DERWENT

PROFESSOR DEXTER FORTESCUE

66 E verard and Dilys were two of Hogwarts's most celebrated Heads. . . . 'Their renown is such that both have portraits hanging in other important wizarding institutions. As they are free to move between their own portraits they can tell us what may be happening elsewhere. . . .' **99**

Order of Merlin

The sword of Gryffindor

The Sorting Hat

Find one matching portrait on page 42

AUTUMN TERM

September 1st Hogwarts school year begins; the Hogwarts Express departs from King's Cross at eleven o'clock; students arrive for the start-of-term feast and the Sorting Ceremony

Tryouts for the house Quidditch teams

Weekend trips to Hogsmeade begin for third years and above if authorized by a parent or guardian

October 31st Halloween feast

Quidditch season begins

Professors and Prefects supervise Christmas decorations

Two weeks before Christmas
Professor McGonagall takes the names of all those wishing to spend Christmas at Hogwarts

Christmas holidays

❝The hall looked spectacular. Festoons of holly and mistletoe hung all around the walls, and no less than twelve towering Christmas trees stood around the room, some sparkling with tiny icicles, some glittering with hundreds of candles.❞

THE SCHOOL YEAR

DRACO DORMIENS NUNQUAM TITILLANDUS

THE SCHOOL SONG

❝'Everyone pick their favorite tune,' said Dumbledore, 'and off we go!'❞

❝'Hogwarts, Hogwarts,
Hoggy Warty Hogwarts,
Teach us something please,
Whether we be old and bald
Or young with scabby knees,
Our heads could do with filling
With some interesting stuff,
For now they're bare and full of air,
Dead flies and bits of fluff,
So teach us things worth knowing,
Bring back what we've forgot,
Just do your best, we'll do the rest,
And learn until our brains all rot.'❞

SPRING
TERM

Third years and above may continue to visit Hogsmeade if they have a permission slip signed by a parent or guardian

February 14th Valentine's Day

"My friendly, card-carrying cupids!' beamed Lockhart. 'They will be roving around the school today delivering your valentines! And the fun doesn't stop here! I'm sure my colleagues will want to enter into the spirit of the occasion! Why not ask Professor Snape to show you how to whip up a Love Potion! And while you're at it, Professor Flitwick knows more about Entrancing Enchantments than any wizard I've ever met, the sly old dog!'"

Apparition lessons for students aged seventeen and older

Easter holidays
Second years choose which subjects to take in third year; fifth years begin career advice ahead of choosing their N.E.W.T. subjects

SUMMER
TERM

"The Gryffindor-Slytherin match would take place on the first Saturday after the Easter holidays. Slytherin was leading the tournament by exactly two hundred points. This meant (as Wood constantly reminded his team) that they needed to win the match by more than that amount to win the Cup."

Weekend trips to Hogsmeade for third years and above if authorized by a parent or guardian

Quidditch final
Awarding of the Inter-House Quidditch Cup

End-of-year exams
O.W.L.s for fifth years and N.E.W.T.s for seventh years

End-of-term feast
Awarding of the House Cup

School year finishes
Hogwarts Express departs from Hogsmeade station

Summer holidays
(O.W.L. and N.E.W.T. results will be sent by owl in July)

To Harry...

From Hagrid

From Uncle Vernon and Aunt Petunia

From Mrs. Weasley

From Hermione

From Dumbledore

We received your message and enclose your Christmas present.

From Kreacher

Have a Very Harry Christmas

BANG!

Non-explodable, luminous balloons

From Fred and George

From Mrs. Weasley

From Dobby

The Fat Lady

Sir Cadogan

Christmas Dinner

The Portraits

GROW-YOUR-OWN-WARTS

The Yule Ball

The Great Hall at Christmas

Bertie Bott's Every Flavor Beans

From Mrs. Weasley

From Ron

From Tonks

From Hagrid

Practical Defensive Magic and its Use Against the Dark Arts

From Sirius and Lupin

From Hermione

From the Dursleys

From Hagrid

FLYING with the CANNONS CC

From Ron

From Hermione

From Mrs. Weasley

From Fred and George

THE MARAUDER'S MAP

From Mrs. Weasley

Snowball Fights

Dobby

Professor Flitwick

BANG!

From Sirius

From Dobby

The Decorations

Crookshanks

NG!

From Mrs. Weasley

From Hagrid

From Sirius

DUNG BOMB

From Ron

QUIDDITCH TEAMS of BRITAIN and IRELAND

From Hermione

From the Dursleys

THE HOUSE CUP

House points in Harry's first year

Gemstones fly down to the bottom of the hourglass when points are awarded, and fly back up when points are taken away.

KEY POINTS AWARDED/TAKEN BY ... ○ SNAPE ● MCGONAGALL ● DUMBLEDORE

*"'*W*hile you are at Hogwarts, your triumphs will earn your House points, while any rule-breaking will lose House points. At the end of the year, the House with the most points is awarded the House Cup, a great honor. I hope each of you will be a credit to whichever House becomes yours.'"*

PROFESSOR MCGONAGALL

116

-1 **HARRY,** *for talking back to the teacher in his first Potions class*

-1 **HARRY,** *blamed for Neville's mistake in their first Potions class*

+? **HERMIONE,** *for knowing about Switching Spells*

-5 **HERMIONE,** *for claiming she went looking for a mountain troll*

+5 **HARRY,** *for taking on the troll*

+5 **RON,** *for taking on the troll*

HALLOWEEN
5 points: lost
10 points: won
Lifelong friendship: gained

-5 **HARRY,** *for taking a library book outside*

-5 **RON,** *for fighting back after Draco Malfoy insults him*

-50 **HARRY,** *for going up the Astronomy Tower at one o'clock in the morning*

But no one discovered that they were really smuggling a baby dragon out of Hogwarts

-50 **HERMIONE,** *for going up the Astronomy Tower at one o'clock in the morning*

DRACO, *for wandering around in the middle of the night* **-20**

-50 **NEVILLE,** *for leaving the dormitory to warn them that they might get caught*

312 Tally at the end-of-year feast **472**

+50 **RON,** *for the best-played game of chess Hogwarts has seen in many years*

+50 **HERMIONE,** *for the use of cool logic in the face of fire*

They got away with going to the third-floor corridor on the right-hand side!

+60 **HARRY,** *for pure nerve and outstanding courage*

+10 **NEVILLE,** *for showing bravery by standing up to his friends*

The House Cup is awarded at the end-of-year feast, when the Great Hall is decorated with the colors and banner of the winning House.

482 Final Gryffindor tally

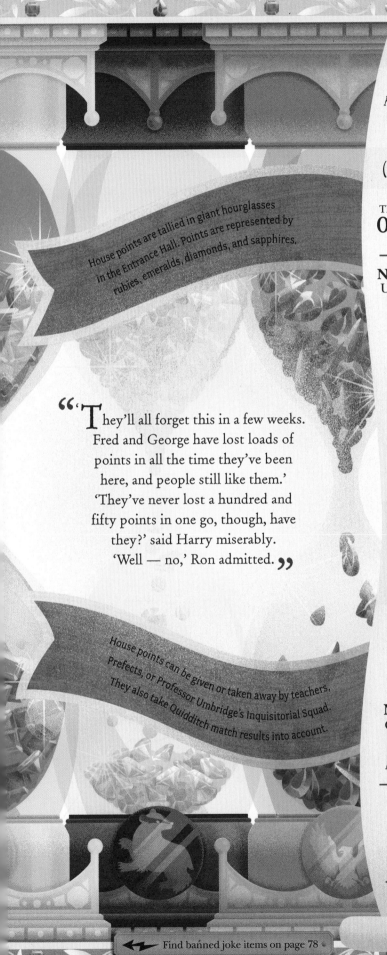

House points are tallied in giant hourglasses in the Entrance Hall. Points are represented by rubies, emeralds, diamonds, and sapphires.

> " 'They'll all forget this in a few weeks. Fred and George have lost loads of points in all the time they've been here, and people still like them.'
> 'They've never lost a hundred and fifty points in one go, though, have they?' said Harry miserably.
> 'Well — no,' Ron admitted. "

House points can be given or taken away by teachers, Prefects, or Professor Umbridge's Inquisitorial Squad. They also take Quidditch match results into account.

PREFECTS

☞ *Prefects are expected to enforce school rules,* patrol the corridors, and guide students to dormitories when needed.

☞ *Privileges include their own carriage on the Hogwarts Express and a special bathroom with a chandelier and diving board.*

(A FEW) SCHOOL RULES**

THE FORBIDDEN FOREST IS **OUT OF BOUNDS** TO ALL PUPILS

HOGSMEADE VISITS ARE **NOT PERMITTED** FOR ANY STUDENTS BELOW THIRD YEAR

NO MAGIC SHOULD BE USED BETWEEN CLASSES IN THE CORRIDORS

THIRD YEARS may only visit on certain weekends, and *MUST* hand in a signed permission form

STUDENTS **MAY NOT** ROAM AROUND THE CASTLE AT NIGHT

FIFTH YEARS AND ABOVE are allowed to be out in the corridors until nine o'clock

BOYS AREN'T ALLOWED IN THE GIRLS' DORMITORY, BUT GIRLS **ARE** ALLOWED IN THE BOYS'

This old-fashioned rule goes back to the days of the Hogwarts founders

FIRST YEARS ARE **NOT** ALLOWED THEIR **OWN BROOMSTICKS**

LOVE POTIONS ARE **BANNED** AT HOGWARTS

117

In Harry's first year

THE THIRD-FLOOR CORRIDOR ON THE RIGHT-HAND SIDE IS **OUT OF BOUNDS** TO EVERYONE WHO DOES NOT WISH TO **DIE A *VERY* PAINFUL DEATH**

THE ASTRONOMY TOWER IS **OUT OF BOUNDS** OUTSIDE OF CLASSES

NO STUDENT MAY LEAVE SCHOOL WITHOUT PERMISSION
While Dementors are guarding Hogwarts in Harry's third year

LIBRARY BOOKS ARE **NOT TO BE TAKEN** OUTSIDE THE SCHOOL

A rule that Professor Snape probably made up just for Harry

THERE IS A BLANKET **BAN** ON ANY JOKE ITEMS BOUGHT AT WEASLEYS' WIZARD WHEEZES

MANY OBJECTS ARE FORBIDDEN INSIDE THE CASTLE, ALL NAMED ON A LIST IN MR. FILCH'S OFFICE OR FASTENED TO HIS DOOR

By Harry's fourth year there are 437 items on the list, including Screaming Yo-yos, Fanged Frisbees, and Ever-Bashing Boomerangs

Even if their siblings are Fred and George Weasley.

**Exceptions are allowed in special cases, such as when students are in detention or become the youngest member of their Quidditch team.*

⚡ Find banned joke items on page 78 ⚡

Mr. Moony presents his compliments to Professor Snape, and begs him to keep his abnormally large nose out of other people's business.

REMUS LUPIN

MOONY

If someone tries to reveal what's hidden without the correct "password," the map will insult them and tell them to mind their own business.

HOGSMEADE

THE MAP SHOWS THE WHOLE OF HOGWARTS, INCLUDING ITS MANY SHORT CUTS AND SECRET PASSAGEWAYS. IT REVEALS THE PEOPLE INSIDE THE CASTLE AS TINY LABELED DOTS, MOVING AROUND THE CORRIDORS.

"It's just a pity they let the old punishments die out . . . hang you by your wrists from the ceiling for a few days, I've got the chains still in my office, keep 'em well oiled in case they're ever needed. . . ."
MR. FILCH

The Marauder's Map was originally plotted by James Potter, Sirius Black, Remus Lupin, and Peter Pettigrew.

Mrs. Norris

Argus Filch

Messrs
MOONY,
WORMTAIL,
PADFOOT, and PRONGS
Purveyors of Aids to Magical Mischief-Makers
are proud to present

"I solemnly swear

that I am up to no good."

HOGSMEADE

"Dissendium"

Harry Potter

IT SHOWS SEVEN SECRET PASSAGES LEADING OUT OF THE SCHOOL. MR. FILCH KNOWS ABOUT FOUR OF THEM, ONE HAS CAVED IN COMPLETELY, THE OTHER TWO LEAD TO THE SHRIEKING SHACK AND THE BASEMENT OF HONEYDUKES IN HOGSMEADE.

WORMTAIL
PETER PETTIGREW

HOGSMEADE

THE MAP CAN STILL BE READ EVEN IF IT IS FAR AWAY FROM HOGWARTS.

Mr. Wormtail bids Professor Snape good day, and advises him to wash his hair, the slimeball.

PRONGS

JAMES POTTER

HOGSMEADE

HOGSMEADE

"Mischief managed!"

TROPHY ROOM

Peeves

THE MARAUDER'S MAP

"Moony, Wormtail, Padfoot, and Prongs,' sighed George, patting the heading of the map. 'We owe them so much.'"

"What would your head have been doing in Hogsmeade, Potter?' said Snape softly. 'Your head is not allowed in Hogsmeade. No part of your body has permission to be in Hogsmeade.'"

THE ROOM OF REQUIREMENT AND THE CHAMBER OF SECRETS DO NOT APPEAR ON THE MAP.

"Wandering around at midnight, Ickle Firsties? Tut, tut, tut. Naughty, naughty, you'll get caughty.'"
PEEVES

THE MARAUDER'S MAP NEVER LIES; EVEN IF YOU ARE WEARING AN INVISIBILITY CLOAK, OR ARE OTHERWISE DISGUISED, YOU WILL ALWAYS APPEAR ON THE MAP AS YOUR TRUE SELF.

"A single dot was flitting around a room in the bottom left-hand corner — Snape's office. But the dot wasn't labeled Severus Snape . . . it was Bartemius Crouch."

Bartemius Crouch

PADFOOT SIRIUS BLACK

HOGSMEADE

Professors and Subjects

"He's off ter the finest school of witchcraft and wizardry in the world. Seven years there and he won't know himself. He'll be with youngsters of his own sort, fer a change, an' he'll be under the greatest headmaster Hogwarts ever had.'"

RUBEUS HAGRID

Professor
Albus Dumbledore
-HEADMASTER-

(Order of Merlin, First Class, Grand Sorc., Chf. Warlock, Supreme Mugwump, International Confed. of Wizards)

"It is our choices, Harry, that show what we truly are, far more than our abilities."

"I can teach you how to bottle fame, brew glory, even stopper death — if you aren't as big a bunch of dunderheads as I usually have to teach."

Professor
Minerva McGonagall
DEPUTY HEADMISTRESS, HEAD OF GRYFFINDOR HOUSE
-TRANSFIGURATION-

"You will excuse me if I don't let you off homework today. I assure you that if you die, you need not hand it in."

Professor
Severus Snape
HEAD OF SLYTHERIN HOUSE
-POTIONS-

Professor
Filius Flitwick
HEAD OF RAVENCLAW HOUSE
-CHARMS-

"Swish and flick, remember, swish and flick."

Professor
Pomona Sprout
HEAD OF HUFFLEPUFF HOUSE
-HERBOLOGY-

"Be careful of the Venomous Tentacula, it's teething."

Professor
Sybill Trelawney
-DIVINATION-

"One does not parade the fact that one is All-Knowing."

Madam
Rolanda Hooch
-QUIDDITCH-

Professor
Cuthbert Binns
HISTORY OF -MAGIC-
GHOST TEACHER

Professor
Rubeus Hagrid
CARE OF MAGICAL -CREATURES-

"Don' be silly, I wouldn' give yeh anythin' dangerous!"

Professor
Quirinus Quirrell
~~DEFENSE AGAINST THE DARK ARTS~~

SEE NEXT

Professor
Horace Slughorn

-POTIONS-

Mr. Wilkie Twycross

-APPARITION INSTRUCTOR-
(MINISTRY OF MAGIC)

"Destination,
Determination, Deliberation!"

Professor
Firenze

-DIVINATION-

Professor
Wilhelmina
Grubbly-Plank

SUBSTITUTE
-TEACHER-

Professor
Bathsheda Babbling

-ANCIENT RUNES-

Professor
Aurora Sinistra

-ASTRONOMY-

Professor
Charity Burbage
-MUGGLE STUDIES-

Professor
Alecto Carrow
-MUGGLE STUDIES-

Professor
Septima Vector
-ARITHMANCY-

"I DUNNO,
DO I?
SHUT IT!"

Professor
Amycus Carrow
DEFENSE AGAINST
-THE DARK ARTS-

NOW

Mrs. Norris

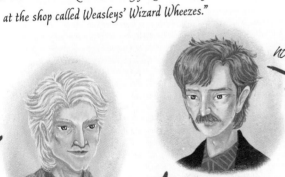

Mr. Argus Filch

SCHOOL
-CARETAKER-

Madam
Irma Pince

SCHOOL
-LIBRARIAN-

Madam
Poppy Pomfrey

-SCHOOL NURSE-

Professor
Severus Snape

DEFENSE AGAINST
-THE DARK ARTS-

NOW
IT IS

"Mr. Filch, our caretaker, has asked me to say
that there is a blanket ban on any joke items bought
at the shop called Weasleys' Wizard Wheezes."

NOW IT IS

Professor
Alastor
"Mad-Eye" Moody

DEFENSE AGAINST
-THE DARK ARTS-

"CONSTANT
VIGILANCE!"

AND NOW

"HEM, HEM."

Professor
Dolores Umbridge

DEFENSE AGAINST
-THE DARK ARTS-

Professor
Remus Lupin

DEFENSE AGAINST
-THE DARK ARTS-
NEW
ONE

Professor
Gilderoy Lockhart

DEFENSE AGAINST
-THE DARK ARTS-

POTIONS

"Professor Snape was forcing them to research antidotes. They took this seriously, as he had hinted that he might be poisoning one of them before Christmas to see if their antidote worked."

DEFENSE AGAINST THE DARK ARTS

"Homework — compose a poem about my defeat of the Wagga Wagga Werewolf! Signed copies of *Magical Me* to the author of the best one!"

PROFESSOR LOCKHART

ROONIL WAZLIB

"'What kind of quill are you using?'
'It's one of Fred and George's Spell-Checking ones . . . but I think the charm must be wearing off. . . .'
'Yes, it must,' said Hermione, pointing at the title of his essay, 'because we were asked how we'd deal with Dementors, not "Dugbogs," and I don't remember you changing your name to "Roonil Wazlib," either.'"

HOMEWORK at HOGWARTS

A magical collection of assignments that can only be found at Hogwarts

YOUR HOMEWORK FOR THE WEEK . . . .

- "*Witch Burning in the Fourteenth Century Was Completely Pointless — discuss*"

- "*Explain Why Muggles Need Electricity*"

- "*Describe, with examples, the ways in which Transforming Spells must be adapted when performing Cross-Species Switches*"

- *Twelve inches of parchment on the properties of moonstone and its uses in potion-making*

- *A foot-and-a-half-long essay on giant wars*

- *An essay on "The Principles of Rematerialization"*

"If you've dotted the i's and crossed the t's then you may do whatever you please!"

"Do it today or later you'll pay!"

"Don't leave it till later, you big second-rater!"

DIVINATION

"'Right,' said Harry, crumpling up his first attempt and lobbing it over the heads of a group of chattering first years into the fire. 'Okay . . . on Monday, I will be in danger of — er — burns.'
'Yeah, you will be,' said Ron darkly, 'we're seeing the skrewts again on Monday. Okay, Tuesday, I'll . . . erm . . .'
'Lose a treasured possession,' said Harry, who was flicking through *Unfogging the Future* for ideas.
'Good one,' said Ron, copying it down. 'Because of . . . erm . . . Mercury. Why don't you get stabbed in the back by someone you thought was a friend?'
'Yeah . . . cool . . .' said Harry, scribbling it down, 'because . . . Venus is in the twelfth house.'
'And on Wednesday, I think I'll come off worst in a fight.'
'Aaah, I was going to have a fight. Okay, I'll lose a bet.'
'Yeah, you'll be betting I'll win my fight. . . .'"

HISTORY OF MAGIC

"Harry found Ron at the back of the library, measuring his History of Magic homework. Professor Binns had asked for a three-foot long composition on 'The Medieval Assembly of European Wizards.'"

DUELING CLUB

A short-lived club set up by Professor Gilderoy Lockhart, which ended when a student conjured a snake; Professor Lockhart accidentally threw it ten feet into the air and the subsequently enraged snake almost attacked the students.

THE SLUG CLUB

Professor Horace Slughorn's club of handpicked students who he believes will go on to illustrious careers; has some very interesting former members.

CHARMS CLUB

For students to practice their charm spells.

GOBSTONES CLUB

A wizarding game rather like marbles, in which the stones squirt a nasty-smelling liquid into the other player's face when they lose a point.

TEAMS, CLUBS, AND SOCIETIES*

123

S.P.E.W.

Hermione's Society for the Promotion of Elfish Welfare.

"I thought two Sickles to join — that buys a badge — and the proceeds can fund our leaflet campaign. You're treasurer, Ron — I've got you a collecting tin upstairs — and Harry, you're secretary, so you might want to write down everything I'm saying now, as a record of our first meeting.' **"**

QUIDDITCH

Each Hogwarts House has its own Quidditch team and they compete during the school year for the Inter-House Quidditch Cup.

"'THIRTY–ZERO! TAKE THAT, YOU DIRTY, CHEATING —'
'Jordan, if you can't commentate in an unbiased way —!'
'I'm telling it like it is, Professor!'**"**

GRYFFINDOR HOUSE QUIDDITCH TEAM 1991

Oliver Wood (Captain) — *Keeper*
Angelina Johnson — *Chaser*
Alicia Spinnet — *Chaser*
Katie Bell — *Chaser*
Fred Weasley — *Beater*
George Weasley — *Beater*
Harry Potter — *Seeker*

MATCH HIGHLIGHTS: GRYFFINDOR VERSUS SLYTHERIN
1991

- Slytherin Captain nearly kills Gryffindor Seeker; penalty awarded to Gryffindor

- Gryffindor Seeker's broom is bewitched; Slytherin Captain seizes the Quaffle and scores five times while no one is looking

- Gryffindor Seeker catches the Snitch in his mouth and nearly swallows it

- Gryffindor wins by one hundred and seventy points to sixty

*Due to the unfortunate events that occurred following Herbology professor Herbert Beery's attempt to introduce a Christmas pantomime of *The Fountain of Fair Fortune* to Hogwarts' festive celebrations, there has been a blanket ban on future pantomimes. It is a proud non-theatrical tradition that continues to this day. Professor Beery eventually left Hogwarts to teach at W.A.D.A. (Wizarding Academy of Dramatic Arts).

Find the rules of Quidditch on page 60

THE HOGWARTS LIBRARY

> "Harry — I think I've just understood something! I've got to go to the library!"
>
> HERMIONE GRANGER

- GILDEROY LOCKHART'S GUIDE TO HOUSEHOLD PESTS
- *Break with a Banshee* — GILDEROY LOCKHART
- *Gadding with Ghouls* — GILDEROY LOCKHART
- *Holidays with Hags* — GILDEROY LOCKHART
- *Travels with Trolls* — GILDEROY LOCKHART
- *Voyages with Vampires* — GILDEROY LOCKHART
- *Wanderings with Werewolves* — GILDEROY LOCKHART
- *Year with the Yeti* — GILDEROY LOCKHART
- MAGICAL ME — GILDEROY LOCKHART

GILDEROY LOCKHART

- ANCIENT RUNES Made Easy
- MAGICAL HIEROGLYPHS AND LOGOGRAMS
- SPELLMAN'S SYLLABARY

LANGUAGE, LINGUISTICS, AND LOGOGRAPHS

- THE DARK FORCES: A GUIDE TO SELF-PROTECTION — QUENTIN TRIMBLE
- DEFENSIVE MAGICAL THEORY — WILBERT SLINKHARD
- *Practical Defensive Magic and its Use Against the Dark Arts*
- CONFRONTING THE FACELESS
- A COMPENDIUM OF COMMON CURSES AND THEIR COUNTER-ACTIONS
- SELF-DEFENSIVE SPELLWORK
- THE DARK ARTS OUTSMARTED
- JINXES FOR THE JINXED

DEFENSE AND DEFENSIVE SPELLS

- UNFOGGING THE FUTURE — CASSANDRA VABLATSKY
- *The Dream Oracle* — INIGO IMAGO
- BROKEN BALLS: WHEN FORTUNES TURN FOUL
- DEATH OMENS: WHAT TO DO WHEN YOU KNOW THE WORST IS COMING
- *Predicting the Unpredictable: Insulate Yourself Against Shocks*

DIVINATION

- QUIDDITCH THROUGH THE AGES — KENNILWORTHY WHISP
- WHICH BROOMSTICK?
- THE BEATERS' BIBLE
- *Flying with the Cannons* — BRUTUS SCRIMGEOUR
- QUIDDITCH TEAMS OF BRITAIN AND IRELAND
- HANDBOOK OF DO-IT-YOURSELF BROOMCARE

SPORT

- HOGWARTS: A History
- A HISTORY OF MAGIC
- An Anthology of Eighteenth-Century CHARMS
- A GUIDE TO MEDIEVAL SORCERY — BATHILDA BAGSHOT
- MODERN MAGICAL HISTORY
- NATURE'S NOBILITY: A Wizarding Genealogy
- *The Rise and Fall of THE DARK ARTS*
- GREAT WIZARDING EVENTS of the TWENTIETH CENTURY
- PREFECTS WHO GAINED POWER
- A STUDY OF RECENT DEVELOPMENTS IN WIZARDRY
- IMPORTANT MODERN MAGICAL DISCOVERIES
- NOTABLE MAGICAL NAMES OF OUR TIME
- GREAT WIZARDS OF THE TWENTIETH CENTURY

MAGICAL HISTORIES

THE ROOM OF
REQUIREMENT

> "It is a room that a person can only enter,' said Dobby seriously, 'when they have real need of it. Sometimes it is there, and sometimes it is not, but when it appears, it is always equipped for the seeker's needs.'"

DOBBY

> "Dobby has used it, sir,' said the elf, dropping his voice and looking guilty, 'when Winky has been very drunk. He has hidden her in the Room of Requirement.'"

PROFESSOR DUMBLEDORE

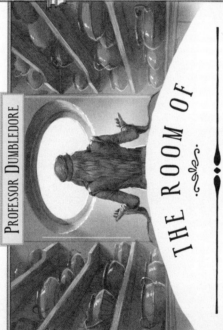

> "Possibly it is only accessible at five-thirty in the morning. Or it may only appear at the quarter moon — or when the seeker has an exceptionally full bladder.'"

MR. FILCH

> "Dobby knows Mr. Filch has found extra cleaning materials there when he has run short, sir.'"

FRED & GEORGE WEASLEY

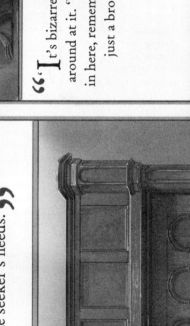

> "It's bizarre,' said Fred, frowning around at it. 'We once hid from Filch in here, remember, George? But it was just a broom cupboard then.'"

PROFESSOR TRELAWNEY

> "I wished to — ah — deposit certain — um — personal items in the room...'"

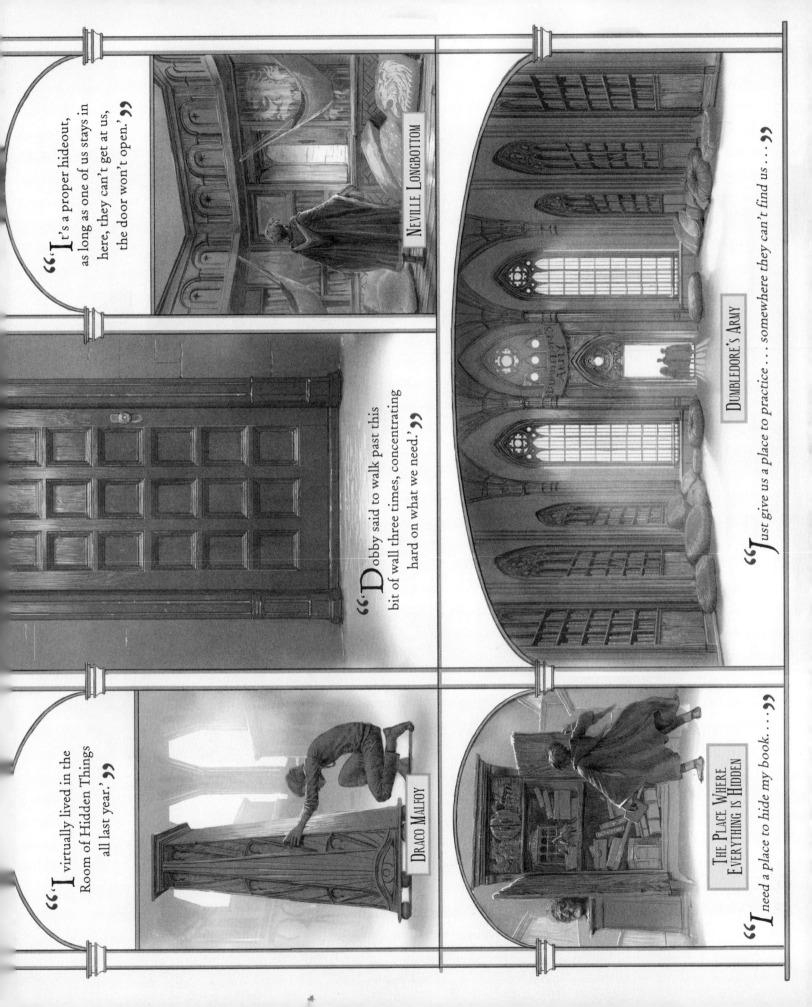

"It's a proper hideout, as long as one of us stays in here, they can't get at us, the door won't open.'

NEVILLE LONGBOTTOM

"Dobby said to walk past this bit of wall three times, concentrating hard on what we need.'

DUMBLEDORE'S ARMY

"Just give us a place to practice ... somewhere they can't find us ...'

"I virtually lived in the Room of Hidden Things all last year.'

DRACO MALFOY

THE PLACE WHERE EVERYTHING IS HIDDEN

"I need a place to hide my book....'

THE DA: A TIMELINE

AUGUST 30, 1995
The Ministry of Magic appoints Dolores Umbridge as Defense Against the Dark Arts teacher at Hogwarts.

SEPTEMBER 2, 1995
Professor Umbridge's first Defense Against the Dark Arts lesson. She denies Lord Voldemort is returning to power and has no intention of teaching students to defend themselves.

SEPTEMBER 1995
Professor Umbridge becomes Hogwarts High Inquisitor.

SEPTEMBER 1995
Hermione suggests they start learning Defense Against the Dark Arts themselves, with Harry as their teacher.

SEPTEMBER/OCTOBER 1995
Harry agrees to teach Defense Against the Dark Arts to his peers.

Hermione suggests they plan a meeting for anyone interested in learning defensive magic outside of lessons.

DUMBLEDORE'S ARMY

In their fifth year, Harry and his friends start a secret study group for Defense Against the Dark Arts.

" 'It's about preparing ourselves, like Harry said in Umbridge's first lesson, for what's waiting out there. It's about making sure we really can defend ourselves.' "

HERMIONE GRANGER

" '*Expelliarmus!*' "   " '*Expecto Patronum!*' "

HARRY POTTER

HERMIONE GRANGER

RON WEASLEY

DUMBLEDORE'S ARMY MEMBERS

Harry Potter
Hermione Granger
Ron Weasley
Neville Longbottom
Ginny Weasley
Luna Lovegood
Dean Thomas
Lavender Brown
Parvati Patil
Padma Patil
Cho Chang
Marietta Edgecombe
Katie Bell
Alicia Spinnet
Angelina Johnson
Colin Creevey
Dennis Creevey
Ernie Macmillan
Justin Finch-Fletchley
Hannah Abbott
Susan Bones
Anthony Goldstein
Michael Corner
Terry Boot
Zacharias Smith
Fred Weasley
George Weasley
Lee Jordan

They agree to take Defense lessons from Harry once a week and sign their names on a list to agree to keep the meetings secret.

IT'S IN THE NAME

By calling themselves "the DA," members can talk about their meetings without revealing what they're up to.

NO SNEAKS

All members sign a piece of parchment. It's jinxed so that if anyone tells Professor Umbridge about the DA, purple pustules will spell out the word "SNEAK" on their face.

THE PERFECT HIDEOUT

Lessons take place in the Room of Requirement.

> "Let's make it stand for Dumbledore's Army because that's the Ministry's worst fear, isn't it?'
>
> GINNY WEASLEY

EDUCATIONAL DECREE NUMBER 24

Any student found to have formed, or to belong to, an Organization, Society, Team, Group, or Club that has not been approved by the High Inquisitor will be expelled.

> "We take one each, and when Harry sets the date of the next meeting he'll change the numbers on *his* coin, and because I've put a Protean Charm on them, they'll all change to mimic his.'
>
> HERMIONE GRANGER

SECRET MESSAGES

Every member has a fake Galleon. It grows hot whenever the numbers around the edge change to reveal the time and date of the next meeting.

Hermione got the idea from the scars of the Death Eaters the DA opposes. (When every Death Eater's scar burns, they know they must go to Voldemort's side.)

> "Stupefy!'

NEVILLE LONGBOTTOM

LUNA LOVEGOOD

> "Impedimenta!'

GINNY WEASLEY

They vote Harry their leader and choose a name: Dumbledore's Army (or "the DA" for short).

Every member is given a fake Galleon, which communicates the time and date of the next meeting.

129

OCTOBER 1995 – SPRING 1996
The DA has regular secret meetings in the Room of Requirement, in which they practice all sorts of charms, jinxes, and defensive spells.

The DA members keep their Galleons in case they're called upon in the Second Wizarding War…

MISCAST MAGIC

"Professor McGonagall was shouting at someone who, by the sound of it, had turned his friend into a badger. **"**

☛ Ron changes a dinner plate into a mushroom

☛ Hannah Abbott multiplies her ferret into a flock of flamingos

☛ Neville transplants his own ears onto a cactus

☛ Lockhart tries to heal Harry's arm and instead makes the bones disappear

☛ Fred and George use an Aging Potion to get past the Goblet of Fire's Age Line, but end up with long white beards

☛ By the start of his fourth year, Neville has melted six cauldrons

130

QUIDDITCH CHAOS

"'Er — have the Bludgers ever killed anyone?' Harry asked, hoping he sounded offhand. 'Never at Hogwarts.' **"**

☛ **First flying lesson:** Neville falls off his broom and breaks his wrist

☛ **First-year match:** Harry's broom nearly throws him off

☛ **Second-year match:** A Bludger goes berserk and attacks Harry

☛ **Third-year match:** Harry falls fifty feet when Dementors invade the stadium

☛ **Fifth-year practice:** Jack Sloper knocks himself out with his own bat

BACKFIRING ENCHANTMENTS

"'It's okay, Hermione,' said Harry quickly. 'We'll take you up to the hospital wing. Madam Pomfrey never asks too many questions. . . .' **"**

☛ Ron's wand backfires when he uses it on Draco Malfoy, leaving Ron belching slugs

☛ The same wand explodes on Lockhart, causing him to wipe his own memory

☛ Eloise Midgen tries to curse off her pimples and removes her own nose

☛ Cormac McLaggen ends up in the hospital wing after eating Doxy eggs for a bet

☛ Hermione accidentally puts cat hair in her Polyjuice Potion and grows fur and pointed ears

MAGICAL MISHAPS

THE WHOMPING WILLOW'S VICTIMS

"'I noticed, in my search of the park, that considerable damage seems to have been done to a very valuable Whomping Willow,' Snape went on.

'That tree did more damage to us than we —' Ron blurted out.

'Silence!' snapped Snape again. **"**

Arthur Weasley's Ford Anglia, beaten up

Harry's Nimbus Two Thousand, smashed to bits

Harry and Hermione, hit by branches while chasing Ron

At last, in the summer of 1998, Ron manages to freeze the tree and get past it

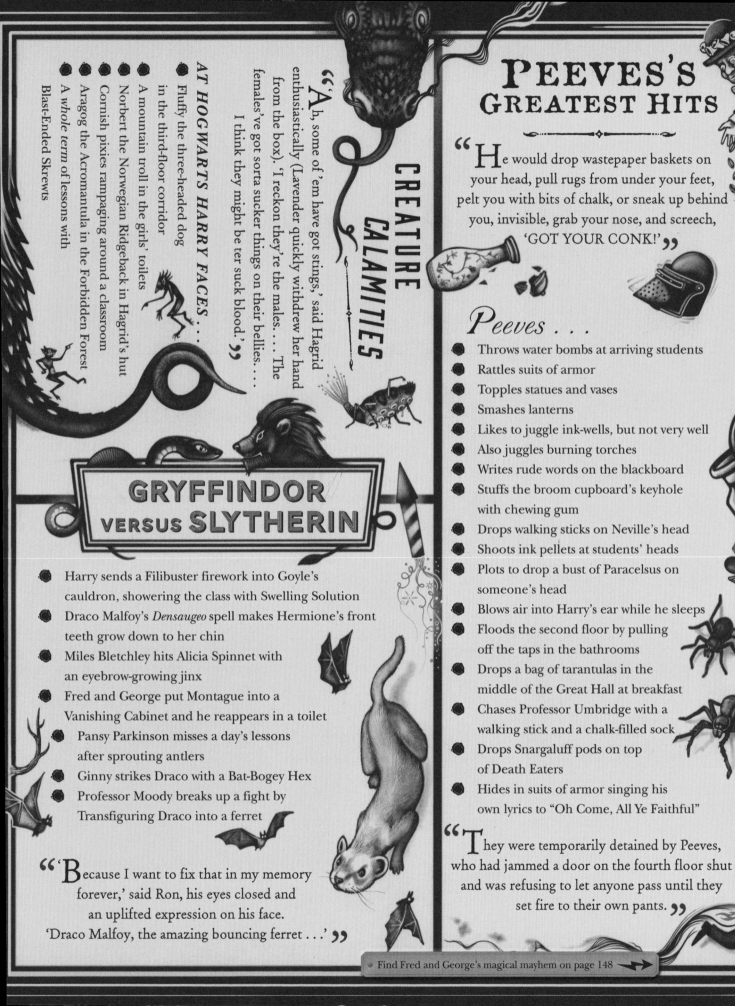

PEEVES'S GREATEST HITS

"He would drop wastepaper baskets on your head, pull rugs from under your feet, pelt you with bits of chalk, or sneak up behind you, invisible, grab your nose, and screech, 'GOT YOUR CONK!'"

Peeves . . .

- Throws water bombs at arriving students
- Rattles suits of armor
- Topples statues and vases
- Smashes lanterns
- Likes to juggle ink-wells, but not very well
- Also juggles burning torches
- Writes rude words on the blackboard
- Stuffs the broom cupboard's keyhole with chewing gum
- Drops walking sticks on Neville's head
- Shoots ink pellets at students' heads
- Plots to drop a bust of Paracelsus on someone's head
- Blows air into Harry's ear while he sleeps
- Floods the second floor by pulling off the taps in the bathrooms
- Drops a bag of tarantulas in the middle of the Great Hall at breakfast
- Chases Professor Umbridge with a walking stick and a chalk-filled sock
- Drops Snargaluff pods on top of Death Eaters
- Hides in suits of armor singing his own lyrics to "Oh Come, All Ye Faithful"

"They were temporarily detained by Peeves, who had jammed a door on the fourth floor shut and was refusing to let anyone pass until they set fire to their own pants."

CREATURE CALAMITIES

"'Ah, some of 'em have got stings,' said Hagrid enthusiastically (Lavender quickly withdrew her hand from the box). 'I reckon they're the males. . . . The females've got sorta sucker things on their bellies. . . . I think they might be ter suck blood.'"

AT HOGWARTS HARRY FACES . . .

- Fluffy the three-headed dog in the third-floor corridor
- A mountain troll in the girls' toilets
- Norbert the Norwegian Ridgeback in Hagrid's hut
- Cornish pixies rampaging around a classroom
- Aragog the Acromantula in the Forbidden Forest
- A whole term of lessons with Blast-Ended Skrewts

GRYFFINDOR VERSUS SLYTHERIN

- Harry sends a Filibuster firework into Goyle's cauldron, showering the class with Swelling Solution
- Draco Malfoy's *Densaugeo* spell makes Hermione's front teeth grow down to her chin
- Miles Bletchley hits Alicia Spinnet with an eyebrow-growing jinx
- Fred and George put Montague into a Vanishing Cabinet and he reappears in a toilet
- Pansy Parkinson misses a day's lessons after sprouting antlers
- Ginny strikes Draco with a Bat-Bogey Hex
- Professor Moody breaks up a fight by Transfiguring Draco into a ferret

"'Because I want to fix that in my memory forever,' said Ron, his eyes closed and an uplifted expression on his face. 'Draco Malfoy, the amazing bouncing ferret . . .'"

Find Fred and George's magical mayhem on page 148 ➔

5

SPELLS, CHARMS, AND UNFORGIVABLE CURSES

From the Patronus Charm to Time-Turners, the shadows of Dark Magic to the silvery enchantment of the Pensieve — magic can be found in many forms. Read up on wandlore, repeat incantations, and learn about the art of potion-making. Pore over a collection of magical objects that fit in your pocket, and hone your knowledge of Defense Against the Dark Arts, Transfiguration, Charms, and Divination.

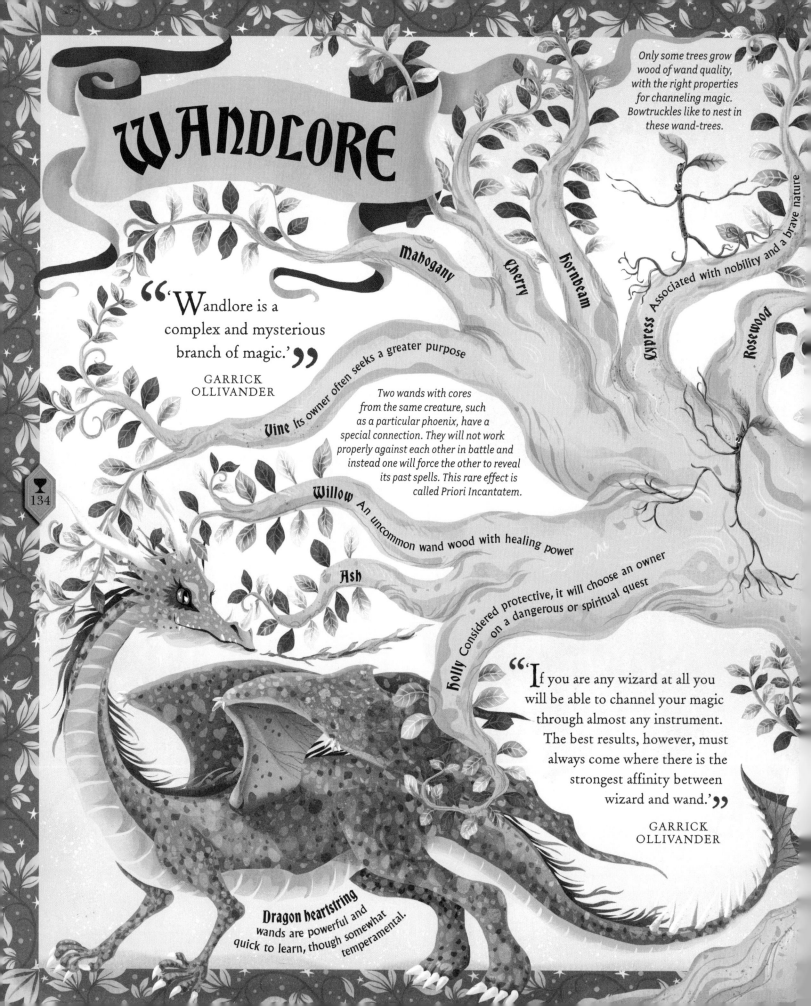

WANDLORE

> "'Wandlore is a complex and mysterious branch of magic.'"
>
> GARRICK OLLIVANDER

Only some trees grow wood of wand quality, with the right properties for channeling magic. Bowtruckles like to nest in these wand-trees.

Mahogany

Cherry

Hornbeam

Cypress Associated with nobility and a brave nature

Rosewood

Vine Its owner often seeks a greater purpose

Two wands with cores from the same creature, such as a particular phoenix, have a special connection. They will not work properly against each other in battle and instead one will force the other to reveal its past spells. This rare effect is called Priori Incantatem.

Willow An uncommon wand wood with healing power

Ash

Holly Considered protective, it will choose an owner on a dangerous or spiritual quest

> "'If you are any wizard at all you will be able to channel your magic through almost any instrument. The best results, however, must always come where there is the strongest affinity between wizard and wand.'"
>
> GARRICK OLLIVANDER

Dragon heartstring wands are powerful and quick to learn, though somewhat temperamental.

Phoenix feather cores are rare and show the greatest range and initiative. Their allegiance is hard to win.

Hazel

Elder *The rarest wood, its master may have a special destiny*

Oak

Beechwood

Fir *Favors those with strength of purpose*

Maple

Alder

Chestnut

Ebony

Birch

Hawthorn *Will often seek an owner with a conflicted nature*

Walnut

Elm

Yew *Reputed to excel at dueling and curses, its owner is often unusual and sometimes notorious*

Subtle laws govern wand ownership. The wand chooses the wizard, and its allegiance will only switch if the wand believes it has been won by its new owner.

Unicorn hair produces faithful wands with consistent magic, which tend to have less power but are hard to use for the Dark Arts.

Every wand is unique

Its character first depends upon its combination of materials and qualities: wood, core, length, and flexibility. Then when it finds its ideal human partner, the two will begin to learn from each other.

Wand woods

Each wood used to make a wand comes with its own properties, depending on the type of tree.

Wand cores

A wand's core is a highly magical substance. It is believed that the finest cores come from the unicorn, dragon, and phoenix.

Length and flexibility

The wand's length and flexibility often complement the witch or wizard's personality and physical attributes.

THE INVISIBILITY CLOAK

Invisibility Cloaks can be created with a Disillusionment Charm or Bedazzling Hex, or woven from the hair of a Demiguise, a creature with invisibility powers. These methods have varying degrees of reliability. Harry's Cloak once belonged to his father.

> "Harry picked the shining, silvery cloth off the floor. It was strange to the touch, like water woven into material.
> 'It's an Invisibility Cloak,' said Ron, a look of awe on his face. 'I'm sure it is — try it on.'"

Your father left this in my possession before he died.
It is time it was returned to you.
Use it well.
A Very Merry Christmas to you.

> "He slipped out of bed and wrapped the Cloak around himself. Looking down at his legs, he saw only moonlight and shadows. It was a very funny feeling.
> *Use it well.*
> Suddenly, Harry felt wide-awake. The whole of Hogwarts was open to him in this Cloak."

Practical

CASTING A SPELL

Most wizards use wands, although wandless magic is possible for those with a lot of talent and skill. There is often an incantation, although with concentration and practice some can learn to cast non-verbal spells.

> "Now, don't forget that nice wrist movement we've been practicing! . . . And saying the magic words properly is very important, too — never forget Wizard Baruffio, who said "s" instead of "f" and found himself on the floor with a buffalo on his chest.'"

PROFESSOR FLITWICK

BROOMSTICK INNOVATIONS
(THEY DO MORE THAN FLY)

Cushioning Charm
Has made broomsticks comfortable since 1820

Horton–Keitch Braking Charm
Aided flight on the Comet 140, an early racing broom

Built-in Warning Whistle
A gimmick on the Twigger 90

Unbreakable Braking Charm
A feature of the Firebolt

Built-in Anti-Burglar Buzzer
Included on the Bluebottle

Anti-jinx varnish
Used on the Cleansweep Eleven

The Bluebottle

A Broom for All the Family —
Safe, Reliable, and with Built-in Anti-Burglar Buzzer

Magic

ACCIO!

'Accio! Accio! Accio!' she shouted, and toffees zoomed from all sorts of unlikely places, including the lining of George's jacket and the turn-ups of Fred's jeans.

The Summoning Charm can be used on a variety of objects:

Ton-Tongue Toffees
Quills
Chairs
An old set of Gobstones
Neville's toad, Trevor
A Rune Dictionary
The Marauder's Map
Harry's Firebolt
A bullfrog

Butterbeer bottles
O.W.L. exam papers
Fred and George's Cleansweep Fives
Harry's wand
Madam Rosmerta's two brooms
Books about Horcruxes
Harry's glasses

MRS. SKOWER'S
All-Purpose
Magical
Mess-Remover
NO PAIN,
NO STAIN!

SOME USEFUL SPELLS

'Point me,' he whispered to his wand, holding it flat in his palm. The wand spun around once, and pointed toward his right, into solid hedge. That way was north, and he knew that he needed to go northwest for the center of the maze.

Open a lock — *Alohomora*
Heal a broken nose — *Episkey*
Cast light from your wand — *Lumos*
Remove unwanted lace from your dress robes — Severing Charm
Mend a smashed bowl — *Reparo*
Breathe from an air bubble while diving — Bubble-Head Charm
Find your way through a maze — Four-Point Spell
Make sure a beetle can't escape from a jar — Unbreakable Charm
Move luggage up the stairs — *Locomotor trunks*
Cast the Leg-Locker Curse — *Locomotor mortis*
Clear your footprints from the snow — Obliteration Charm
Clean blood from your friend's face — *Tergeo*
Bring statues and suits of armor to life — *Piertotum locomotor*
Flatten a staircase into a chute — *Glisseo*
Turn a small beaded handbag into a secret cargo hold — Undetectable Extension Charm

137

CURSES, JINXES, AND HEXES

Curse of the Bogies
Furnunculus Curse
Leg-Locker Curse
Reductor Curse
Body-Bind Curse

Jelly-Legs Jinx
Impediment Jinx
Trip Jinx
Anti-Disapparition Jinx

Backfiring Jinx
Revulsion Jinx
Stinging Jinx (or Hex)
Hurling Hex

Bat-Bogey Hex
Bedazzling Hex
Tickling Charm
(also effective)

138

TERGEO Used for cleaning

COLLOPORTUS Seals a door

LIBERACORPUS The counter-jinx to Levicorpus

LOCOMOTOR Moves inanimate objects

SERPENSORTIA Conjures a snake

RICTUSEMPRA A Tickling Charm

APARECIUM Makes invisible ink visible

MUFFLIATO Fills the ears of anyone nearby with an unidentifiable buzzing

QUIETUS Reverses the Sonorus Charm

PESKIPIKSI PESTERNOMI Not helpful for subduing pixies

IMPEDIMENTA Incantation of the Impediment Jinx; obstructs attackers

LANGLOCK Stops another person (or poltergeist) from speaking

METEOLOJINX RECANTO Worth a try if your office has been raining lately

SCOURGIFY Useful for cleaning

PROTEGO Incantation of the Shield Charm; casts an invisible wall to deflect certain spells

ALOHOMORA Opens locks

SILENCIO Incantation of the Silencing Charm

EXPECTO PATRONUM Incantation of the Patronus Charm; summons a Patronus, a concentrated positive force

ORCHIDEOUS Conjures flowers

WINGARDIUM LEVIOSA Levitates objects; pronounced "Wing-Gar-dium Levi-o-sa, make the 'gar' nice and long."

FURNUNCULUS Causes boils; has interesting side-effects when mixed with the Jelly-Legs Jinx

OPPUGNO Directs an object to attack

MISCHIEF MANAGED Makes the Marauder's Map disappear; accompanied by a light tap of the wand on the parchment

LEVICORPUS Dangles the subject upside down in midair by their ankle

ENGORGIO Incantation of the Engorgement Charm; makes an object swell up

MOBILICORPUS Good for moving an unconscious body

REDUCIO Reverses the effects of an Engorgement Charm

FINITE INCANTATEM Causes an earlier spell to cease

RIDDIKULUS Makes a Boggart take on a comical appearance

MORSMORDRE Conjures the Dark Mark

DENSAUGEO Causes teeth to grow

ANAPNEO Stops someone choking

EXPULSO Blows up objects

INCANTATIONS

For best results, casting a spell requires both the right incantation and the right wand movements. Advanced magic uses non-verbal spells, giving the element of surprise...

INCENDIO Creates fire

FLAGRANTI Good for dislodging chewing gum

ERECTO Builds or constructs

EXPELLIARMUS Incantation of the Disarming Charm

REPARO Repairs an object

LUMOS Ignites a wand-tip with light

FLAGRATE Creates a fiery mark

NOX Extinguishes wandlight

GEMINO Duplicates an object

OBLIVIATE Makes the subject forget

CONFUNDO Incantation of the Confundus Charm; confuses the victim

EPISKEY Heals injuries

DIFFINDO Makes something split or break apart

DISSENDIUM Opens the entrance to a secret passage

FERULA Conjures a splint for a broken limb

PRIOR INCANTATO Reveals the most recent spell a wand has performed

RENNERVATE Revives another

PETRIFICUS TOTALUS Incantation of the immobilizing Body-Bind Curse

STUPEFY Incantation of the Stunning Spell; stuns another and can render them unconscious

AGUAMENTI A water-making charm

I SOLEMNLY SWEAR THAT I AM UP TO NO GOOD Makes the Marauder's Map reveal itself

ACCIO Incantation of the Summoning Charm; calls an object to you

OBSCURO Temporarily obscures another's eyesight

DURO Turns objects to stone

REDUCTO Incantation of the Reductor Curse; blasts apart a solid object

RELASHIO Breaks someone free from chains or another's grip

SECTUMSEMPRA "For Enemies"; leads to extreme blood loss

TARANTALLEGRA Compels someone to dance rapidly

AVIS Conjures a flock of small birds

DESCENDO Pulls objects down from a height

SONORUS Magnifies one's voice

HOMENUM REVELIO Reveals human presence; accompanied by tapping the parchment with a wand

PORTUS Transforms an object into a Portkey

139

Some curses are Unforgivable; find out more on page 157

CHARMS

"Professor Flitwick, the Charms teacher, was a tiny little wizard who had to stand on a pile of books to see over his desk."

'Swish and flick, remember, swish and flick.'
PROFESSOR FLITWICK

Locomotion Charm
Growth Charm
Cheering Charm
Color Change Charm

᚛ Levitation Charm ᚜
Makes an object float

✳ *Wingardium Leviosa!* ✳

"'You're saying it wrong . . . It's Wing-*gar*-dium Levi-*o*-sa, make the "gar" nice and long.'"

HERMIONE
GRANGER

᚛ Summoning Charm ᚜
Makes any object fly through the air toward you; it works whether or not you know where the object is

✳ *Accio!* ✳

"Harry pointed his wand at the bullfrog that had been hopping hopefully toward the other side of the table — '*Accio!*' — and it zoomed gloomily back into his hand."

GRADE 4

THE
STANDARD
BOOK OF
SPELLS

BY
MIRANDA
GOSHAWK

᚛ Aguamenti Charm ᚜
Conjures water from the wand

✳ *Aguamenti!* ✳

"He flicked his wand a little too enthusiastically, so that instead of producing the fountain of pure water that was the object of today's Charms lesson, he let out a hoselike jet that ricocheted off the ceiling and knocked Professor Flitwick flat on his face."

᚛ Banishing Charm ᚜
The opposite of the Summoning Charm

✳ *Depulso!* ✳

"He Banished a cushion with a sweep of his wand (it soared into the air and knocked Parvati's hat off)."

᚛ Silencing Charm ᚜
Stops something, such as a croaking raven, from producing sound

✳ *Silencio!* ✳

"'It's the way you're moving your wand,' said Hermione, watching Ron critically. 'You don't want to wave it, it's more a sharp *jab*.'"

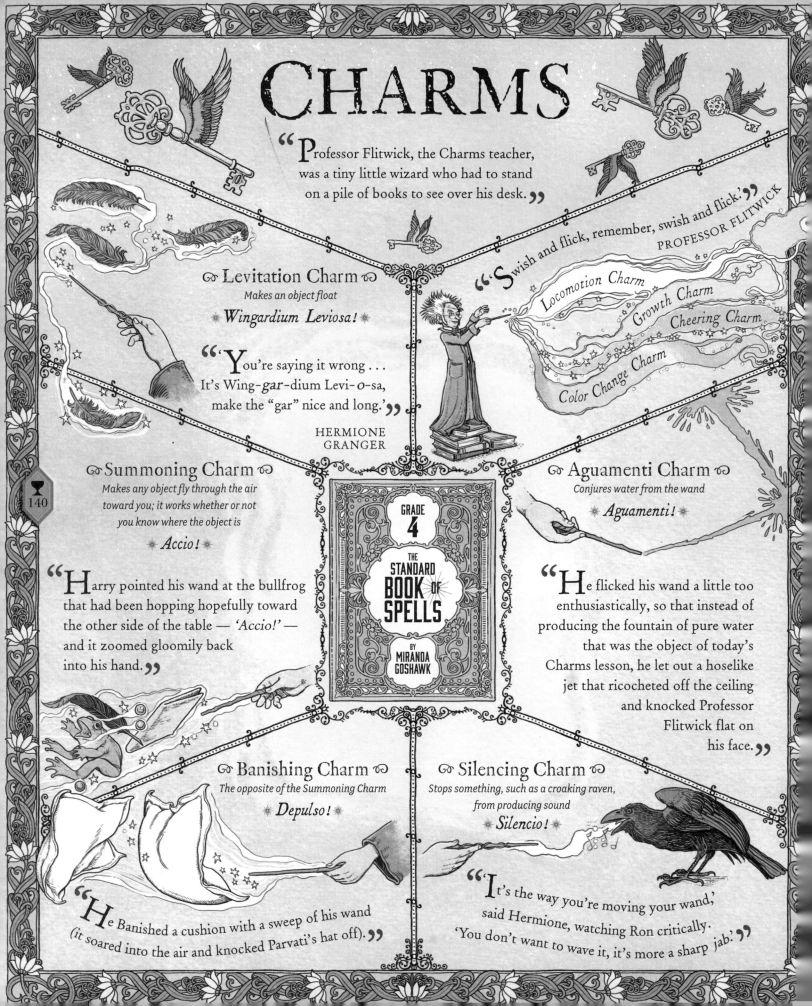

Divination

"In fact, it didn't look like a classroom at all, more like a cross between someone's attic and an old-fashioned tea shop . . . . A voice came suddenly out of the shadows, a soft, misty sort of voice. 'Welcome,' it said. 'How nice to see you in the physical world at last.'"

Palmistry

"'Don't complain, this means we've finished palmistry,' Harry muttered back. 'I was getting sick of her flinching every time she looked at my hands.'"

Reading Tea Leaves

"'Sit down and drink, drink until only the dregs remain. Swill these around the cup three times with the left hand, then turn the cup upside down on its saucer, wait for the last of the tea to drain away. . . .'"

PROFESSOR TRELAWNEY

CROSS
Trials and suffering

SUN
Great happiness

ACORN
A windfall, unexpected gold

THE GRIM
Death

FALCON
A deadly enemy

CLUB
An attack

SKULL
Danger in your path

Planetary Divination

"'Today, however, will be an excellent opportunity to examine the effects of Mars, for he is placed most interestingly at the present time. If you will all look this way, I will dim the lights. . . .'"

PROFESSOR TRELAWNEY

"'Lie back upon the floor,' said Firenze in his calm voice, 'and observe the heavens. Here is written, for those who can see, the fortune of our races.'"

Crystal-Gazing

"'I do not expect any of you to See when first you peer into the Orb's infinite depths. We shall start by practicing relaxing the conscious mind and external eyes.'"

PROFESSOR TRELAWNEY

Dream Interpretation

"'Okay, we've got to add your age to the date you had the dream . . . would the number of letters in the subject . . . that be "drowning" or "cauldron" or "Snape"?'"

RON WEASLEY

The Dream Oracle
INIGO IMAGO

Transfiguration

"Professor McGonagall was again different. Harry had been quite right to think she wasn't a teacher to cross. Strict and clever, she gave them a talking-to the moment they had sat down in her first class."

Fourth year

Transforming Spells, Switching Spells, Cross-Species Switches

First year

CHANGE A MATCH INTO A NEEDLE

Third year

TURN A TEAPOT INTO A TORTOISE

SWITCH A CACTUS

MISTAKES TO AVOID: *transplanting your own ears onto a cactus*

CHANGE GUINEA-FOWL INTO GUINEA-PIGS

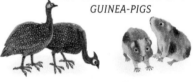

MISTAKES TO AVOID: *the guinea-pig still having feathers*

Second year

TURN A BEETLE INTO A BUTTON

MISTAKES TO AVOID: *letting the beetle scuttle away; accidentally squashing it*

MISTAKES TO AVOID: *a spout for a tail; a willow-patterned shell; a tortoise that looks more like a turtle*

142

Animagi

Animagi are wizards who can transform at will into animals.

It takes years to become an Animagus. Those who succeed can only ever take on one animal form, which they cannot choose or change.

———❖———

There is a register for all Animagi at the Ministry of Magic, in the Improper Use of Magic Office.

———❖———

The Ministry only recorded seven Animagi in Britain in the twentieth century, although there were others who were unregistered.

Rita Skeeter

"Inside were a few twigs and leaves and one large, fat beetle."

Peter Pettigrew

"Even Pettigrew's voice was squeaky. Again, his eyes darted toward the door."

Fifth year

Vanishing Spells, Inanimatus Conjurus Spell

VANISH SNAILS

MISTAKES TO AVOID:
leaving some shell remaining

VANISH MICE

VANISH KITTENS

O.W.L. exam
VANISH AN IGUANA

"'The Vanishing Spell becomes more difficult with the complexity of the animal to be vanished. The snail, as an invertebrate, does not present much of a challenge; the mouse, as a mammal, offers a much greater one.'"

PROFESSOR MCGONAGALL

Intermediate Transfiguration
TURN AN OWL INTO A PAIR OF OPERA GLASSES

Sixth year

Conjuring Spells,
Human Transfiguration

CONJURE TWITTERING YELLOW BIRDS

CHANGE THE COLOR OF YOUR OWN EYEBROWS

MISTAKES TO AVOID: *giving yourself a spectacular handlebar mustache*

143

Minerva McGonagall

"'Fancy seeing you here, Professor McGonagall.' He turned to smile at the tabby, but it had gone. Instead he was smiling at a rather severe-looking woman who was wearing square glasses exactly the shape of the markings the cat had had around its eyes."

Sirius Black

"The enormous, bearlike dog bounded forward."

James Potter

"Slowly, it bowed its antlered head. And Harry realized . . ."

POTIONS

> **"**'I don't expect you will really understand the beauty of the softly simmering cauldron with its shimmering fumes, the delicate power of liquids that creep through human veins, bewitching the mind, ensnaring the senses. . . .'**"**
>
> PROFESSOR SNAPE

> **"**Potions lessons took place down in one of the dungeons. It was colder here than up in the main castle and would have been quite creepy enough without the pickled animals floating in glass jars all around the walls.**"**

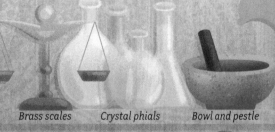

Brass scales   *Crystal phials*   *Bowl and pestle*

SCARAB BEETLES

GINGER ROOTS

Bezoars

ARMADILLO BILE

WIT-SHARPENING POTION

Ingredients:

- Scarab beetles, crushed to a fine powder
- Ginger roots, sliced
- Armadillo bile

144

POLYJUICE POTION

- Gives you the physical appearance of another person
- Thick and mudlike, it changes color depending on who you change into
- Produces sluggish bubbles
- Can go very wrong if brewed incorrectly

VERITASERUM

- Forces the drinker to tell the truth
- Colorless
- Odorless
- Powerful and controlled by Ministry guidelines

All potion brewing has an element of wandwork.

A naked flame is essential.

Commonly made of pewter or iron, cauldrons are also available in solid gold for show-offs. All cauldrons are enchanted so they're lighter to carry, and can also be self-stirring or collapsible.

HOW TO BREW
THE DRAUGHT OF LIVING DEATH

This potion takes about an hour to brew

Add powdered root of asphodel to an infusion of wormwood

Chop up valerian roots

Cut up the sopophorous bean

Advice from the Half-Blood Prince:

Crush with flat side of silver dagger, releases juice better than cutting.

Stir counter-clockwise until the potion turns clear as water

Advice from the Half-Blood Prince:

Add a clockwise stir after every seventh counterclockwise stir

Within ten minutes, the cauldron will give off bluish steam

At the halfway stage, the ideal potion is smooth and black currant–colored

After adding enough sopophorous bean juice, the potion turns a light shade of lilac

First the potion will turn pink, then finally clear

Final Potion Colors

EXCELLENT

CLEARLY WRONG

> " A crackling from under the rim told Harry they had lit a fire beneath it. Conjuring up portable, waterproof fires was a speciality of Hermione's. "

> " For your information, Potter, asphodel and wormwood make a sleeping potion so powerful it is known as the Draught of Living Death. "
>
> PROFESSOR SNAPE

> " Amortentia doesn't really create *love*, of course. It is impossible to manufacture or imitate love. No, this will simply cause a powerful infatuation or obsession.' "
>
> PROFESSOR SLUGHORN

AMORTENTIA

- Causes a strong infatuation
- Mother-of-pearl sheen
- Has a different attractive smell for each person
- Its steam rises in spirals
- The obsession it creates can be very dangerous

ADVANCED POTION-MAKING

LIBATIUS BORAGE

145

FELIX FELICIS

- Provides good luck while its effects last, giving it the name "liquid luck"
- The color of molten gold
- Drops splash around merrily without spilling
- Too much can cause recklessness and overconfidence

Defense Against the Dark Arts

"Troll — in the dungeons — thought you ought to know."
He then sank to the floor in a dead faint.

"They had never yet had a Defense Against the Dark Arts teacher who had lasted more than three terms."

"Boggarts like dark, enclosed spaces," said Professor Lupin.
'Wardrobes, the gap beneath beds, the cupboards under sinks . . . but when I let him out, he will immediately become whatever each of us most fears.'

"I must ask you not to scream," said Lockhart in a low voice. 'It might provoke them.'
As the whole class held its breath, Lockhart whipped off the cover.
'Yes,' he said dramatically.
'Freshly caught Cornish pixies.'

FIFTH YEAR
Dolores Umbridge

"Using defensive spells?' Professor Umbridge repeated with a little laugh. 'Why, I can't imagine any situation arising in my classroom that would require you to use a defensive spell, Miss Granger. You surely aren't expecting to be attacked during class?'"

"You know what it's like, Hagrid told us, nobody wants the job; they say it's jinxed.'"

HARRY POTTER

SEVENTH YEAR
Amycus Carrow

"Amycus, the bloke, he teaches what used to be Defense Against the Dark Arts, except now it's just the Dark Arts.'"

NEVILLE LONGBOTTOM

FOURTH YEAR
Mad-Eye Moody

"Moody reached into the jar, caught one of the spiders, and held it in the palm of his hand so that they could all see it. He then pointed his wand at it, and muttered, 'Imperio!'"

"One sacked, one dead, one's memory removed, and one locked in a trunk for nine months,' said Harry, counting them off on his fingers."

"You will now divide,' Snape went on, 'into pairs. One partner will attempt to jinx the other without speaking. The other will attempt to repel the jinx in equal silence. Carry on.'"

SIXTH YEAR
Severus Snape

MASTERS of MAYHEM

Fred and George Weasley may not be top of the class, but their magical pranks are legendary.

1989–1990

Finding the Marauder's Map

"'Well . . . when we were in our first year, Harry — young, carefree, and innocent —' Harry snorted. He doubted whether Fred and George had ever been innocent. '— well, more innocent than we are now — we got into a spot of bother with Filch.'

. . .

'— and we couldn't help noticing a drawer in one of his filing cabinets marked *Confiscated and Highly Dangerous*.'

'Don't tell me —' said Harry, starting to grin.

'Well, what would you've done?' said Fred. 'George caused a diversion by dropping another Dungbomb, I whipped the drawer open and grabbed — *this*.'"

• DECEMBER • 1991

1987–1988

Acid Pops

"'Fred gave me one of those when I was seven — it burnt a hole right through my tongue.'"

RON WEASLEY

1983–1984

Ron's Teddy Bear

"'If you must know, when I was three, Fred turned my teddy bear into a great big filthy spider because I broke his toy broomstick.'"

RON WEASLEY

Snowball Fight

"The Weasley twins were punished for bewitching several snowballs so that they followed Quirrell around, bouncing off the back of his turban."

• JUNE • 1992

A Toilet Seat

"'I believe your friends Misters Fred and George Weasley were responsible for trying to send you a toilet seat. No doubt they thought it would amuse you.'"

ALBUS DUMBLEDORE

Pinhead Percy

"Percy, who hadn't noticed that Fred had bewitched his prefect badge so that it now read 'Pinhead,' kept asking them all what they were sniggering at."

• DECEMBER • 1992

• AUGUST • 1994

Ton-Tongue Toffee

"'You dropped it on purpose!' roared Mr. Weasley. 'You knew he'd eat it, you knew he was on a diet —'

'How big did his tongue get?' George asked eagerly.

'It was four feet long before his parents would let me shrink it!'"

• SEPTEMBER • 1994

Fooling the Goblet of Fire

"There was a loud sizzling sound, and both twins were hurled out of the golden circle as though they had been thrown by an invisible shot-putter. They landed painfully, ten feet away on the cold stone floor, and to add insult to injury, there was a loud popping noise, and both of them sprouted identical long white beards."

GRYFFINDOR

Wildfire Whiz-Bangs

"Somebody (and Harry had a very shrewd idea who) had set off what seemed to be an enormous crate of enchanted fireworks. Dragons comprised entirely of green-and-gold sparks were soaring up and down the corridors, emitting loud fiery blasts and bangs as they went. Shocking-pink Catherine wheels five feet in diameter were whizzing lethally through the air like so many flying saucers. Rockets with long tails of brilliant silver stars were ricocheting off the walls. Sparklers were writing swearwords in midair of their own accord. Firecrackers were exploding like mines everywhere. . . ."

A Portable Swamp

"'So — you think it amusing to turn a school corridor into a swamp, do you?' 'Pretty amusing, yeah,' said Fred, looking back up at her without the slightest sign of fear."

Discover Weasleys' Wizard Wheezes on page 78

Ride into the Sunset

"Peeves, whom Harry had never seen take an order from a student before, swept his belled hat from his head and sprang to a salute as Fred and George wheeled about to tumultuous applause from the students below and sped out of the open front doors into the glorious sunset."

149

Extendable Ears

"'Time is Galleons, little brother,' said Fred. 'Anyway, Harry, you're interfering with reception. Extendable Ears,' he added in response to Harry's raised eyebrows, holding up the string, which Harry now saw was trailing out onto the landing. 'We're trying to hear what's going on downstairs.'"

A Monument to Fred and George

"Well, Flitwick's got rid of Fred and George's swamp,' said Ginny. 'He did it in about three seconds. But he left a tiny patch under the window and he's roped it off —'
'Why?' said Hermione, looking startled.
'Oh, he just says it was a really good bit of magic,' said Ginny, shrugging.
'I think he left it as a monument to Fred and George,' said Ron through a mouthful of chocolate."

✦ MAGICAL OBJECTS THAT FIT IN YOUR POCKET ✦

WIZARDING WATCH

A traditional coming-of-age gift for a wizard

Puts out lights; also stores light inside for later use

DELUMINATOR

REMEMBRALL

Turns red if there's something you've forgotten to do

MINIATURE MODEL DRAGON

Shows Triwizard champions which creature they are about to face

Draco dormiens nunquam titillandus

SORCERER'S STONE

Transforms any metal into pure gold and produces the Elixir of Life

TWO-WAY MIRROR

One of a pair; say someone's name to talk to them through the mirrors

MARAUDER'S MAP

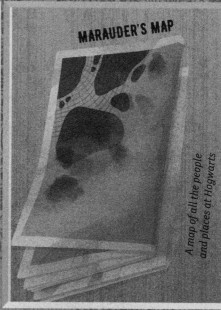

A map of all the people and places at Hogwarts

SPELL-CHECKING QUILL

Improves the writer's spelling

WAND For casting spells

Excellent on everything from boils to blackheads

Guaranteed Ten-Second Pimple Vanisher

NOSE-BITING TEACUP

A teacup that bites noses

A potion for regrowing bones

SKELE-GRO

TIME-TURNER

Sends the wearer back in time; to be used with care

Insert one end into your ear, and you can hear out of the other end

EXTENDABLE EARS

150

 Find more quills on page 40

INVISIBILITY CLOAK

Renders the wearer invisible

FAMOUS WITCHES AND WIZARDS CARD

Collectable and informative, found inside a Chocolate Frog

ALBUS DUMBLEDORE

PORTABLE FLAMES IN A JAR

A speciality of Hermione's; can be used for warmth

GOLDEN SNITCH

A hard ball to catch, requiring perseverance and skill

Liquid luck; drinking it makes you lucky

FELIX FELICIS

Can magnify, replay, and slow down what you see through them

OMNIOCULARS

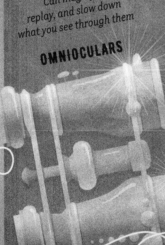

DECOY DETONATOR

Runs away and creates a loud bang and black smoke; good for diversions

Lights up and spins if there's someone untrustworthy around

SNEAKOSCOPE

Eat it and you turn into a large canary for a minute

CANARY CREAM

Crystal-gazing is a particularly refined art; can be an effective weapon when thrown

CRYSTAL BALL

Lets you travel from fireplace to fireplace via the Floo Network

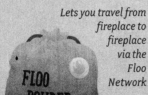

FLOO POWDER

A sweet that makes you smoke at the mouth

PEPPER IMP

FOE-GLASS

Enemies appear in this mirror when they're close by

VERITASERUM

A powerful Truth Potion

DUMBLEDORE'S ARMY GALLEON

Reveals the time and date of DA meetings

↩ Learn about the DA on page 128

WEREWOLVES

A werewolf is a human who transforms once a month when the moon is full.

The condition, known as lycanthropy, is caused when someone is bitten by a transformed werewolf during the full moon.

The beastlike form is nearly indistinguishable from a true wolf, apart from a slightly shorter snout, tufted tail, and smaller pupils.

When untreated, transformed werewolves lose their sense of morality and seek out human prey.

Lycanthropy can afflict Muggles as well as wizardkind and there is no known cure. However, it can be managed with Wolfsbane Potion.

Werewolves are widely distrusted by the wizarding community, although they are ordinary humans on all other days of the month. The Ministry of Magic has a Werewolf Registry, although many werewolves try to hide their condition for fear of becoming outcasts.

NEW MOON

WAXING CRESCENT

WANING CRESCENT

FIRST QUARTER

THIRD QUARTER

WAXING GIBBOUS

WANING GIBBOUS

FULL MOON

"'It makes me safe, you see. As long as I take it in the week preceding the full moon, I keep my mind when I transform. . . . I am able to curl up in my office, a harmless wolf, and wait for the moon to wane again. Before the Wolfsbane Potion was discovered, however, I became a fully fledged monster once a month.'"

REMUS LUPIN

"'Dumbledore's trust has meant everything to me. He let me into Hogwarts as a boy, and he gave me a job when I have been shunned all my adult life, unable to find paid work because of what I am.'"

REMUS LUPIN

152

TIME-TURNERS

A Time-Turner is a small, enchanted hourglass containing a single Hour-Reversal Charm.

It is worn on a chain around the neck and lets the wearer travel into the past.

The Ministry of Magic gives Hermione permission to use a Time-Turner during her third year at Hogwarts, to help her attend several lessons at once. But one night she and Harry relive three hours for an entirely different purpose . . .

"**A**re you telling me,' Harry whispered, 'that we're here in this cupboard and we're out there too?'"

To use a Time-Turner, the wearer must turn over the hourglass. For every time the hourglass is turned, the wearer will go back one hour.

Going back in time is extremely dangerous. Time-Turners can be borrowed from the Ministry of Magic, but there are hundreds of laws restricting how they can be used.

They leave the Entrance Hall and go outside

Harry, Ron, and Hermione decide to go to Hagrid's hut at sunset

Harry and Hermione hide in a cupboard by the Entrance Hall

Harry, Ron, and Hermione arrive at Hagrid's

They go to Hagrid's hut and hide outside, close to where Buckbeak is tethered

Hagrid drops his milk jug and it shatters on the floor

Harry and Hermione arrive in the Entrance Hall three hours earlier

They hear the crash of Hagrid breaking the milk jug

Harry, Ron, and Hermione leave Hagrid's and see Buckbeak tied to a tree in the garden

After watching their past selves leave Hagrid's, they free Buckbeak when no one's looking

They encounter Sirius in his Animagus form

From a distance, they watch their earlier encounter with Sirius

Lupin transforms into a werewolf

After Lupin transforms, they hide from him in Hagrid's hut

Harry and Hermione run to the lake after Sirius, where they're attacked by Dementors

Harry runs toward the lake and the attacking Dementors

Harry sees someone cast a Patronus to chase away the Dementors

Harry succeeds in casting a corporeal Patronus

Snape floats the unconscious Harry, Hermione, Ron, and Sirius back to the castle

Hermione and Buckbeak join Harry by the lake and wait for the right moment to rescue Sirius

Sirius is locked inside Flitwick's office

"**H**ermione turned the hourglass over three times."

Harry and Hermione ride Buckbeak and fly up to the office where Sirius is being held

Harry and Hermione wake up in the hospital wing

Together they fly to the top of the West Tower

Dumbledore arrives and suggests they can redo the previous three hours

Hermione reveals the Time-Turner to Harry and places the chain around their necks

With only ten minutes to spare, they return to the hospital wing

"**B**ut remember this, both of you: *You must not be seen.*'"
ALBUS DUMBLEDORE

Dumbledore leaves Harry and Hermione alone in the infirmary

Harry and Hermione return to their hospital beds

They meet Dumbledore, who has just left the infirmary

The night continues . . .

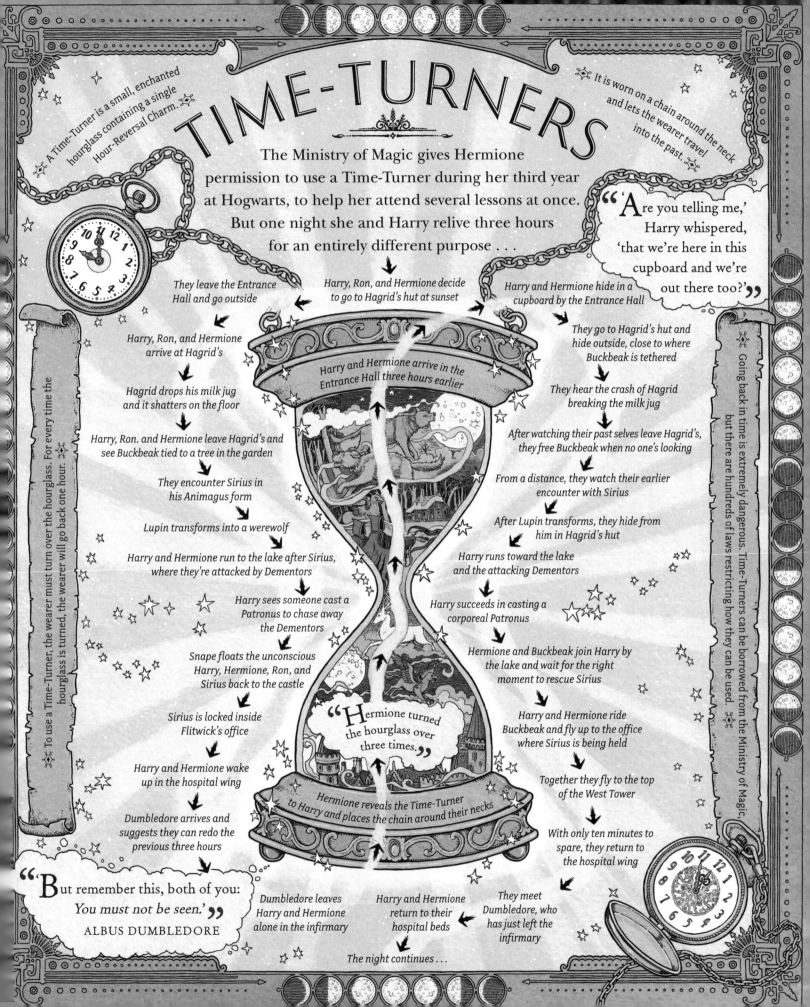

MAGIC
OF THE
MIND

From the enchanted Mirror of Erised
to the power of seeing another's memories,
the magic of the mind can reveal difficult truths.

> "'It does not do to dwell on dreams
> and forget to live, remember that.'"
>
> ALBUS DUMBLEDORE

~ THE MIRROR OF ERISED ~

> "'It shows us nothing more or less than the deepest,
> most desperate desire of our hearts. You, who
> have never known your family, see them standing
> around you. Ronald Weasley, who has always been
> overshadowed by his brothers, sees himself standing
> alone, the best of all of them. However, this mirror
> will give us neither knowledge or truth. Men have
> wasted away before it, entranced by what they
> have seen, or been driven mad, not knowing if
> what it shows is real or even possible.'"
>
> ALBUS DUMBLEDORE

~ OCCLUMENCY AND LEGILIMENCY ~

OCCLUMENCY
is the magical defense of
the mind against external
penetration. An obscure
branch of magic, but a
highly useful one, it seals
the mind against magical
intrusion and influence.

> "'The Dark Lord, for instance, almost
> always knows when somebody is lying to him.
> Only those skilled at Occlumency are able to
> shut down those feelings and memories that
> contradict the lie, and so can utter falsehoods
> in his presence without detection.'"
>
> SEVERUS SNAPE

LEGILIMENCY
is the ability to extract feelings
and memories from another person's
mind. Those who have mastered
Legilimency are able, under certain
conditions, to delve into the minds
of their victims and to interpret
their findings correctly. Eye contact
is often essential to Legilimency;
the incantation is *"Legilimens."*

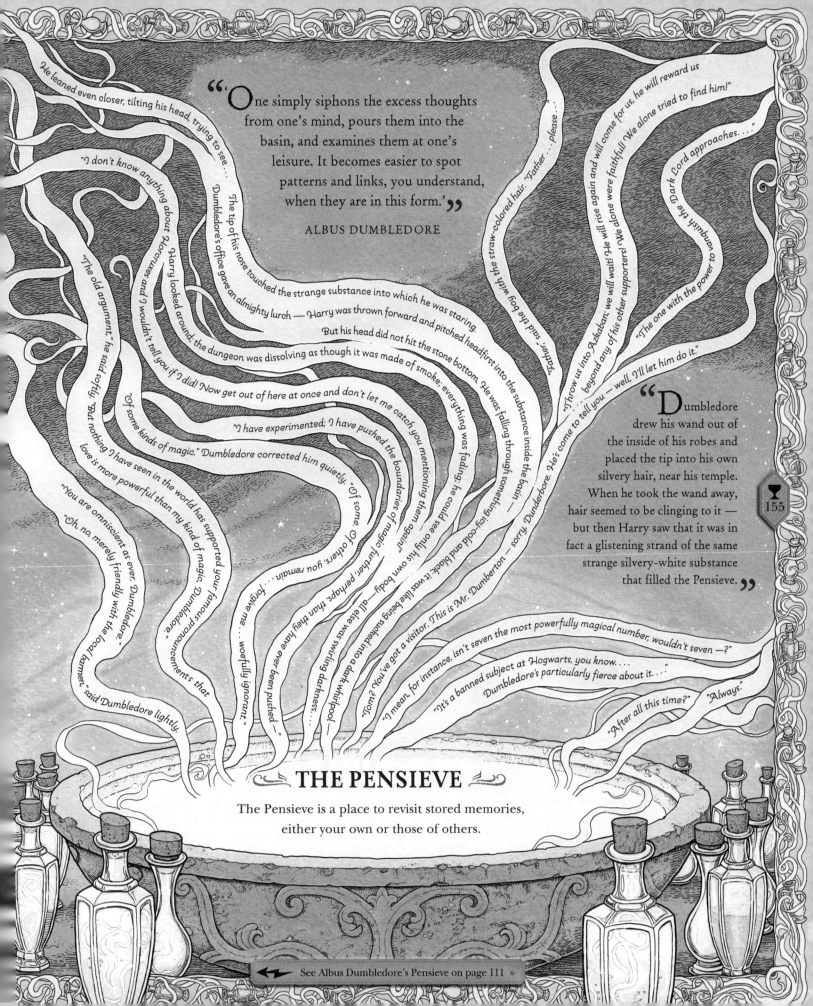

"One simply siphons the excess thoughts from one's mind, pours them into the basin, and examines them at one's leisure. It becomes easier to spot patterns and links, you understand, when they are in this form.'"

ALBUS DUMBLEDORE

"Dumbledore drew his wand out of the inside of his robes and placed the tip into his own silvery hair, near his temple. When he took the wand away, hair seemed to be clinging to it — but then Harry saw that it was in fact a glistening strand of the same strange silvery-white substance that filled the Pensieve."

He leaned even closer, tilting his head, trying to see....

"I don't know anything about Horcruxes and I wouldn't tell you if I did! Now get out of here at once and don't let me catch you mentioning them again."

The tip of his nose touched the strange substance into which he was staring. Dumbledore's office gave an almighty lurch — Harry was thrown forward and pitched headfirst into the substance.

But his head did not hit the stone bottom. He was falling through something icy-cold and black; it was like being sucked into a dark whirlpool — all else was swirling darkness. . . .

"The old argument," he said softly. "But nothing I have seen in the world has supported your famous pronouncements that love is more powerful than my kind of magic."

"I have experimented; I have pushed the boundaries of magic further, perhaps, than they have ever been pushed —"

"Of some kinds of magic," Dumbledore corrected him quietly. "Of some. Of others, you remain . . . woefully ignorant."

"You are omniscient as ever, Dumbledore."

"Oh, no, merely friendly with the local barmen," said Dumbledore lightly.

"Tom? You've got a visitor. This is Mr. Dumberton — sorry, Dunderbore. He's come to tell you —

". . . beyond any of his other supporters! We alone were faithful! We alone tried to find him!"

"Throw us into Azkaban; we will wait! He will rise again and will come for us, he will reward us

"The one with the power to . . ."

". . . the Dark Lord approaches. . . ."

"Father . . ." said the body with the straw-colored hair. "Father . . . please . . ."

"It's a banned subject at Hogwarts, you know. . . . Dumbledore's particularly fierce about it. . . ."

"I mean, for instance, isn't seven the most powerfully magical number, wouldn't seven —?"

"After all this time?" "Always."

155

THE PENSIEVE

The Pensieve is a place to revisit stored memories, either your own or those of others.

See Albus Dumbledore's Pensieve on page 111

DARK MAGIC

Throughout history there have always been practitioners of the Dark Arts. One of the most famous and powerful, of course, is Lord Voldemort.

"'The Dark Arts,' said Snape, 'are many, varied, ever-changing, and eternal. Fighting them is like fighting a many-headed monster, which, each time a neck is severed, sprouts a head even fiercer and cleverer than before. You are fighting that which is unfixed, mutating, indestructible.'"

"'I was ripped from my body, I was less than spirit, less than the meanest ghost . . . but still, I was alive. What I was, even I do not know . . . I, who have gone further than anybody along the path that leads to immortality. You know my goal — to conquer death. And now, I was tested, and it appeared that one or more of my experiments had worked . . .'"

LORD
VOLDEMORT

156

"'He disappeared after leaving the school . . . traveled far and wide . . . sank so deeply into the Dark Arts, consorted with the very worst of our kind, underwent so many dangerous, magical transformations, that when he resurfaced as Lord Voldemort, he was barely recognizable.'"

ALBUS DUMBLEDORE

DEATH EATERS
During the First Wizarding War, Lord Voldemort amassed devoted followers called Death Eaters, who united under the symbol of the Dark Mark.

The Dark Mark is cast into the sky with the incantation "Morsmordre"; Death Eaters use it to spread terror through communities.

Each Death Eater had the Dark Mark burned into their arm by Voldemort himself, as a means of distinguishing them and summoning them to him.

THE UNFORGIVABLE CURSES

There are three Unforgivable Curses;
the use of any one of these is enough
to earn a life sentence in Azkaban.

IMPERIO The incantation of the Imperius Curse: controls another person completely

CRUCIO The incantation of the Cruciatus Curse; inflicts torture

AVADA KEDAVRA The incantation of the Killing Curse; there is no counter-curse and only one known person has ever survived it . . .

"'Sir, I wondered what you
know about . . . about Horcruxes?'
Slughorn froze. His round face seemed
to sink in upon itself. He licked
his lips and said hoarsely,
'What did you say?'"

After Voldemort's defeat in the First Wizarding War, many of his followers went into hiding or claimed to have been under the control of the Imperius Curse to avoid answering for their crimes. Others were sentenced to life in Azkaban, where they awaited their Dark Lord's return.

"'You will hear many of his Death Eaters claiming that they
are in his confidence, that they alone are close to him, even
understand him. They are deluded. Lord Voldemort
has never had a friend, nor do I believe that
he has ever wanted one.'"

ALBUS
DUMBLEDORE

ERNIE
MACMILLAN
Boar

SEAMUS
FINNIGAN
Fox

The Patronus Charm is
highly advanced
magic.

And then a silver hare, a boar, and a fox soared past Harry, Ron, and Hermione's heads: The Dementors fell back before the creatures' approach.'

RON
WEASLEY
*Jack Russell
terrier*

THE PATRONUS

LUNA
LOVEGOOD
Hare

'The Patronus is a kind of positive
force, a projection of the very things
that the Dementor feeds upon —
hope, happiness, the desire to
survive — but it cannot feel despair,
as real humans can, so the
Dementors can't hurt it.'

REMUS LUPIN

'It's a stag,
it's always a stag.'

CHO
CHANG
Swan

'EXPECTO PATRONUM!'

HERMIONE
GRANGER
Otter

HARRY
POTTER
Stag

'It's the only spell she ever has trouble with.'

The incantation will only
work if you are concentrating
with all your might on a single,
very happy memory.

'Prongs,' he whispered.

"It was a silver-white doe, moon-bright and dazzling, picking her way over the ground, still silent, and leaving no hoofprints in the fine powdering of snow."

"It resolved itself into a bright silver weasel, which stood on its hind legs and spoke with Mr. Weasley's voice."

ARTHUR WEASLEY
Weasel

Not all wizards can conjure a corporeal, fully formed Patronus. For some it remains wisps and vapors of silvery mist.

KINGSLEY SHACKLEBOLT
Lynx

ALBUS DUMBLEDORE
Phoenix

Each Patronus is unique to the witch or wizard who conjures it.

159

"Graceful and gleaming, the lynx landed lightly in the middle of the astonished dancers."

NYMPHADORA TONKS
Wolf

ABERFORTH DUMBLEDORE
Goat

"Why would your Patronus change?'"

The form their Patronus takes may change during the course of a witch or wizard's life.

MINERVA McGONAGALL
Cat

"From the tip burst three silver cats with spectacle markings around their eyes."

REMUS LUPIN
Wolf

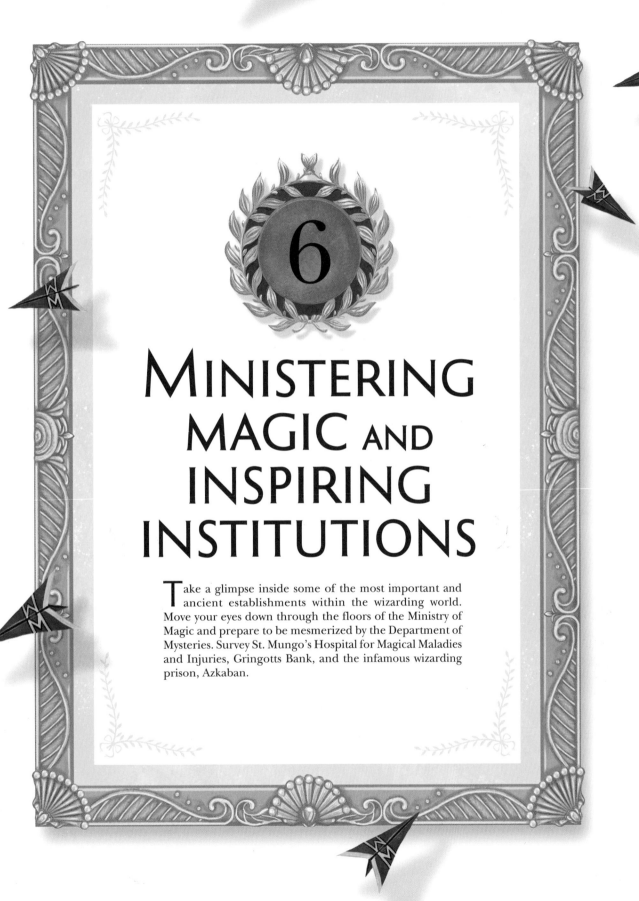

6

MINISTERING MAGIC AND INSPIRING INSTITUTIONS

Take a glimpse inside some of the most important and ancient establishments within the wizarding world. Move your eyes down through the floors of the Ministry of Magic and prepare to be mesmerized by the Department of Mysteries. Survey St. Mungo's Hospital for Magical Maladies and Injuries, Gringotts Bank, and the infamous wizarding prison, Azkaban.

THE MINISTRY OF MAGIC

Formally established in 1707, the Ministry of Magic (M.O.M.) governs the magical community in Britain. Located underground in the heart of London, its chief responsibilities are protecting the wizarding world and keeping it secret from Muggles.

THE MINISTER OF MAGIC

While at Hogwarts, Harry Potter crosses paths with four Ministers: Cornelius Fudge, Rufus Scrimgeour, Pius Thicknesse, and Kingsley Shacklebolt. The first Minister of Magic was Ulick Gamp. His portrait hangs in the Muggle Prime Minister's study and is used for emergency communications with the Muggle world.

⁓ VISITING THE MINISTRY ⁓

VISITORS must enter via a telephone box above the building:

1. Dial 62442
2. State your name and business
3. Receive a silver visitor's badge from the change compartment
4. The telephone box then drops down like a lift into the Atrium

EMPLOYEES enter via fireplaces in the Atrium.
When extra security is needed, employees must enter by flushing themselves down a secret entrance in a public toilet. The toilets are tiled in grimy black and white but the entry tokens are golden.

⁓ AURORS ⁓

Aurors are Dark wizard–catchers. Anyone seeking to become one must:

- Achieve a minimum of five N.E.W.T.s at Exceeds Expectations or above; recommended subjects include Defense Against the Dark Arts, Transfiguration, Charms, and Potions

- Pass stringent character and aptitude tests, covering practical Defense skills and reacting well to pressure

- Take three years of additional training and exams, including Concealment and Disguise, and Stealth and Tracking

" 'I got top marks in Concealment and Disguise during Auror training without any study at all, it was great.' "

NYMPHADORA TONKS

Other magical law enforcement teams include the Magical Law Enforcement Patrol, the Werewolf Capture Unit, and Hit Wizards.

⁓ THE WIZENGAMOT ⁓

The Wizengamot, the Wizard High Court, has been around longer than the Ministry of Magic. Today it functions as both a court and parliament. Wearing plum-colored robes emblazoned with a silver "W," members abide by the Wizengamot Charter of Rights and pass judgment over those suspected of breaking wizarding law. Albus Dumbledore holds the title of Chief Warlock.

162

A teapot that squirts boiling tea

Shrinking door-keys

Sugar tongs that clamp onto your nose

MISUSED MUGGLE ARTIFACTS

Regurgitating toilets

A biting kettle

It is illegal to bewitch everyday Muggle objects and use them, in case it leads to the discovery of magic. Arthur Weasley encounters all sorts of bewitched objects at the Misuse of Muggle Artifacts Office.

THE ORDER OF MERLIN

The Order of Merlin has been awarded by the Wizengamot since the fifteenth century.

FIRST CLASS
FOR ACTS OF OUTSTANDING BRAVERY OR DISTINCTION IN MAGIC

- **Albus Dumbledore** for defeating the Dark wizard Grindelwald
- **Cornelius Fudge** for a distinguished career (self-awarded)
- **Arcturus Black** for unknown reasons (coincidentally after loaning the Ministry a large amount of gold)
- **Peter Pettigrew** for aiding in Sirius Black's arrest

SECOND CLASS
FOR ACHIEVEMENT OR ENDEAVOR BEYOND THE ORDINARY

- **Newt Scamander** for his services to Magizoology, the study of magical beasts

THIRD CLASS FOR THOSE WHO HAVE MADE A CONTRIBUTION TO OUR STORE OF KNOWLEDGE OR ENTERTAINMENT

- **Gilderoy Lockhart** for his unbelievable achievements in literature

- **Damocles Belby** for inventing Wolfsbane Potion (award class unknown)

UPHOLDERS OF THE LAW

"It was an accident! We don't send people to Azkaban just for blowing up their aunts!'"

CORNELIUS FUDGE

The Ministry has passed a multitude of laws and decrees since its establishment:

INTERNATIONAL STATUTE OF SECRECY
(FIRST SIGNED IN 1689, OVERSEEN IN BRITAIN BY THE MINISTRY)

Numerous breaches at the 1994 Quidditch World Cup, when attempts at "an entirely Muggle standard of dress" included a Wimbourne Wasps uniform and a tweed suit with thigh-length galoshes

LAW AGAINST CASTING AN EXTENSION CHARM FOR PRIVATE USE

Broken by Hermione Granger when she charmed a small handbag

DECREE FOR THE REASONABLE RESTRICTION OF UNDERAGE SORCERY

Allegedly broken by Harry Potter for using a Hover Charm; actually broken by Harry Potter for blowing up Marjorie Dursley

BAN ON EXPERIMENTAL BREEDING
(DEVELOPED BY NEWT SCAMANDER IN 1965)

Broken when someone created a fire-breathing chicken

LAW AGAINST ENCHANTING MUGGLE OBJECTS

Not broken by Arthur Weasley when he made a flying car, because of a loophole allowing the enchantment if he didn't intend to use it (but he did actually use an Extension Charm)

163

Find Albus Dumbledore's Order of Merlin on page 111

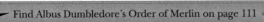

TOUR *the* MINISTRY *of* MAGIC

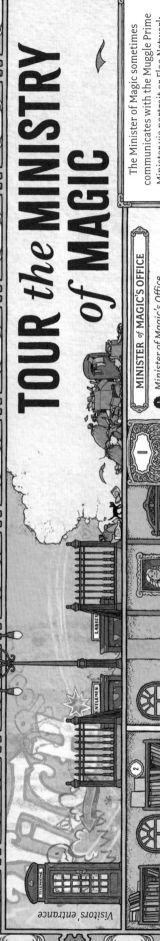

Visitors' entrance

The Minister of Magic sometimes communicates with the Muggle Prime Minister via portrait or Floo Network. No Muggle Minister will ever admit it.

> "Look at it from my point of view . . . I'm under a lot of pressure. Got to be seen to be doing something."
>
> CORNELIUS FUDGE Minister of Magic

1 MINISTER *of* MAGIC'S OFFICE
1. *Minister of Magic's Office*
2. *Support Staff Offices*

> "Of course, it's very hard to convict anyone because no Muggle would admit their key keeps shrinking."
>
> ARTHUR WEASLEY Misuse of Muggle Artifacts Office

2 DEPARTMENT *of* MAGICAL LAW ENFORCEMENT
3. *Auror Headquarters*
4. *Broom Cupboard*
5. *Misuse of Muggle Artifacts Office*
6. *Wizengamot Administration Services*
7. *Improper Use of Magic Office*

Obliviators are specially trained to use Memory Charms to erase or modify the memories of Muggles who may have noticed wizarding activity.

3 DEPARTMENT *of* MAGICAL ACCIDENTS *and* CATASTROPHES
8. *Accidental Magic Reversal Squad*
9. *Obliviator Headquarters*
10. *Office of Misinformation*
11. *Muggle-Worthy Excuse Committee*

---

4 DEPARTMENT *for the* REGULATION *and* CONTROL *of* MAGICAL CREATURES
BEING DIVISION
12. *Dragon Research and Restraint Bureau*
- *Werewolf Capture Unit*
- *Werewolf Register*
- *Ghoul Task Force*
- *Centaur Liaison Office**
- *Pest Advisory Bureau*

13. **BEING DIVISION**
- *Office for House-Elf Relocation*
- *Werewolf Support Services Office*
- *Goblin Liaison Office*

14. **SPIRIT DIVISION**

* *Never used*

> "We're trying to standardize cauldron thickness."
>
> PERCY WEASLEY Department of International Magical Cooperation

5 DEPARTMENT *of* INTERNATIONAL MAGICAL COOPERATION
15. *International Magical Trading Standards Body*
16. *International Magical Office of Law*
17. *International Confederation of Wizards, British Seats*

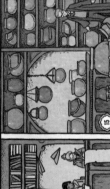

← Learn about Apparition on page 49

IT IS AGAINST THE LAW TO APPARATE WITHOUT A LICENCE

YOU MUST BE AT LEAST SEVENTEEN TO BE ELIGIBLE

DEPARTMENT of MAGICAL TRANSPORTATION

ALL PORTKEYS HAVE TO BE AUTHORIZED BEFORE USE

18 Floo Network Authority
19 Broom Regulatory Control
20 Portkey Office
21 Apparition Test Center

"'It's all happening at Hogwarts now, you know, much more exciting here than at the office!'"

LUDO BAGMAN
Head of Magical Games and Sports

DEPARTMENT of MAGICAL GAMES and SPORTS

This department helped to organize the Triwizard Tournament.

22 British and Irish Quidditch League Headquarters
23 Official Gobstones Club
24 Ludicrous Patents Office

"'Magical Maintenance decide what weather we're getting every day. We had two months of hurricanes last time they were angling for a pay raise. . . .'"

ARTHUR WEASLEY

Enchanted underground windows

Inter-departmental memos swoop and flap around the building

All proceeds from the Fountain of Magical Brethren will be given to St. Mungo's Hospital for Magical Maladies and Injuries.

ATRIUM

25 Security Desk
26 Fountain of Magical Brethren

"'He stepped out into a torch-lit stone passageway quite different from the wood-paneled and carpeted corridors above. As the lift rattled away again, Harry shivered slightly, looking toward the distant black door that marked the entrance to the Department of Mysteries.'"

DEPARTMENT of MYSTERIES

COURTROOMS

The courtrooms are rarely used and can only be accessed by the stairs.

27 Courtroom Ten

The Wizengamot sits on the highest benches in Courtroom Ten. There is enough room to seat the full court of around fifty members.

An enchanted chair binds dangerous criminals in chains during testimony.

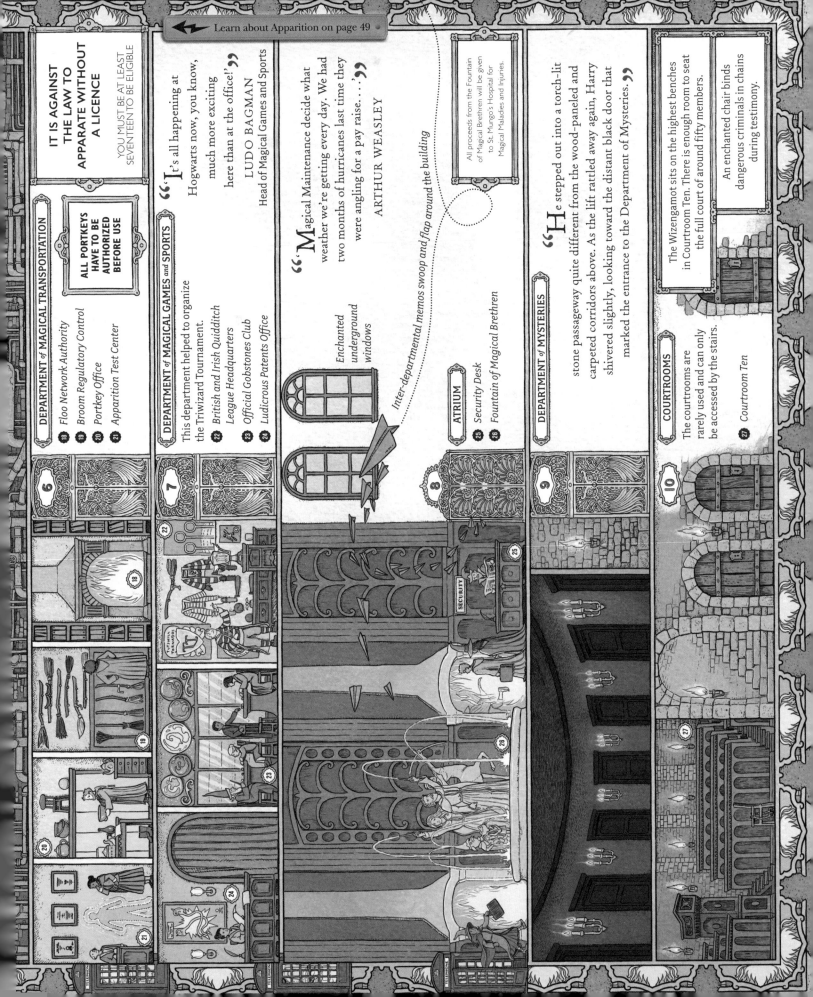

The Department of Mysteries

The ninth floor of the Ministry of Magic is a curious place, where employees known as "Unspeakables" study the biggest mysteries of magic.

"Everything in here was black including the floor and ceiling—identical, unmarked, handle-less black doors were set at intervals all around the black walls, interspersed with branches of candles whose flames burned blue, their cool, shimmering light reflected in the shining marble floor so that it looked as though there was dark water underfoot."

THE CIRCULAR ROOM

"Glimmering eerily they drifted in and out of sight in the depths of the green water, looking something like slimy cauliflowers."

"The veil swayed gently, as though somebody had just passed through it."

THE BRAIN ROOM

THE DEATH CHAMBER

"There is a room in the Department of Mysteries . . . that is kept locked at all times. It contains a force that is at once more wonderful and more terrible than death, than human intelligence, than forces of nature. It is also, perhaps, the most mysterious of the many subjects for study that reside there. It is the power held within that room that you possess in such quantities and which Voldemort has not at all.'

ALBUS DUMBLEDORE

THE LOCKED DOOR

"Drifting along in the sparkling current inside was a tiny, jewel-bright egg. As it rose in the jar, it cracked open and a hummingbird emerged, which was carried to the very top of the jar, but as it fell on the draft, its feathers became bedraggled and damp again, and by the time it had been borne back to the bottom of the jar it had been enclosed once more in its egg."

167

THE TIME ROOM

"They were there, they had found the place: high as a church and full of nothing but towering shelves covered in small, dusty, glass orbs."

S.P.T. to A.P.W.B.D.
Dark Lord
and (?)Harry Potter

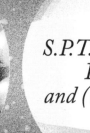

"The others moved in closer around Harry, gazing at the orb as he brushed it free of the clogging dust."

THE HALL OF PROPHECY

ROW NINETY-SEVEN

GRINGOTTS WIZARDING BANK

To visit a vault, customers must bring their key (if they have one), and be escorted down into the tunnels deep below the bank, where the vaults are hidden

THE WEASLEY FAMILY VAULT

"They say there's dragons guardin' the high-security vaults. And then yeh gotta find yer way — Gringotts is hundreds of miles under London, see. Deep under the Underground. Yeh'd die of hunger tryin' ter get out, even if yeh did manage ter get yer hands on summat."

RUBEUS HAGRID

"Griphook unlocked the door. A lot of green smoke came billowing out, and as it cleared, Harry gasped. Inside were mounds of gold coins. Columns of were mounds of gold coins. Heaps of little bronze Knuts."

Visitors here can exchange Muggle money for wizarding currency

"Enter, stranger, but take heed of what awaits the sin of greed. For those who take, but do not earn, must pay most dearly in their turn. So if you seek beneath our floors a treasure that was never yours, thief, you have been warned, beware of finding more than treasure there."

Gringotts is famously located in Diagon Alley

"They were in a narrow stone passageway lit with flaming torches. It sloped steeply downward and there were little railway tracks on the floor. Griphook whistled and a small cart came hurtling up the tracks toward them. They climbed in — Hagrid with some difficulty — and were off."

SIRIUS BLACK'S VAULT

GRINGOTTS BREAK-IN LATEST

INVESTIGATIONS CONTINUE into the break-in at Gringotts on July 31, widely believed to be the work of Dark wizards or witches unknown, insisted today that the vault that Gringotts goblins had been taken. The nothing had in fact been emptied the was searched had in fact been same day. what not telling you if "But we're keep your noses out in there, so said a Gri-know what's good for you," spokesgoblin this afternoon.

THE
POTTER
FAMILY VAULT

THE THIEF'S DOWNFALL

The waterfall washes away all enchantment and magical concealment; ideal for catching impostors

THE
SORCERER'S
STONE

713

"'**S**tand back,' said Griphook importantly. He stroked the door gently with one of his long fingers and it simply melted away."

THE
LESTRANGE
FAMILY VAULT

The oldest wizarding families store their treasures at the deepest level, where the vaults are largest and best protected

THE PRISON OF AZKABAN

In the middle of the North Sea stands the fortress of Azkaban, the wizard prison, home to some of the most notorious members of the wizarding world.

> "'The fortress is set on a tiny island, way out to sea, but they don't need walls and water to keep the prisoners in, not when they're all trapped inside their own heads, incapable of a single cheerful thought. Most of them go mad within weeks.'"
>
> REMUS LUPIN

The island in the North Sea on which Azkaban was built has never appeared on any map, Muggle or magical

Azkaban has existed since the fifteenth century and was originally home to a little-known sorcerer named Ekrizdis, a practitioner of the worst kind of Dark Arts

When Ekrizdis died, the concealment charms around Azkaban faded and the Ministry of Magic discovered its existence

Officials realized the fortress was infested with Dementors, drawn to the misery and pain of the Dark Arts practiced there, and the island was left abandoned for many years

After the enforcement of the International Statute of Secrecy in 1692, an eighteenth-century Minister of Magic, Damocles Rowle, decided to use Azkaban as a remote and well-hidden wizard prison, harnessing the Dementors to act as its guards

DEMENTORS OF AZKABAN

> ❝**D**ementors are among the foulest creatures that walk this earth.❞
>
> REMUS LUPIN

- Dementors are the prison guards of Azkaban; they thrive in dark, filthy places and feed off the despair of those around them

- They are blind and feel their way by feeding on emotions, draining peace, hope, and happiness from their surroundings

- Dementors will not be fooled by tricks, disguises, or even Invisibility Cloaks

> ❝**W**here there should have been eyes, there was only thin, gray scabbed skin, stretched blankly over empty sockets. But there was a mouth . . . a gaping, shapeless hole, sucking the air with the sound of a death rattle.❞

- Too much time with a Dementor will drain a witch or wizard of their magical powers, and almost always causes them to descend into madness

- Anyone in the presence of a Dementor would feel cold to their bones, hear the sound of a rattling breath, and smell a rotting odor; few people have seen the face of a Dementor, for they are always dressed in a hooded cloak, only taking it down to perform a Kiss

- A Kiss is the Dementor's ultimate weapon, which it performs by clamping its jaws upon the mouth of the victim and sucking out their soul

> ❝**L**ong as they've got a couple o' hundred humans stuck there with 'em, so they can leech all the happiness out of 'em, they don' give a damn who's guilty an' who's not.❞
>
> RUBEUS HAGRID

(KNOWN) BREAKOUTS

Officially, according to the Ministry of Magic, there have been virtually no breakouts from Azkaban. However, even the Ministry could not hide the most infamous and daring escape, made single-handedly by Sirius Black in 1993.

> ❝**N**ever been a breakout from Azkaban before, 'as there, Ern? Beats me 'ow 'e did it.❞
>
> STAN SHUNPIKE

BLACK STILL AT LARGE

SIRIUS BLACK, possibly the most infamous prisoner ever to be held in Azkaban fortress, is still eluding capture, the Ministry of Magic confirmed today.

"We are doing all we can to recapture Black," said the Minister of Magic, Cornelius Fudge, this morning, "and we beg the magical community to remain calm."

Fudge has been criticized by some members of the International Federation of Warlocks for informing the Muggle Prime Minister of the crisis.

"Well, really, I had to, don't you know," said an irritable Fudge. "Black is mad. He's a danger to anyone who crosses him, magic or Muggle. I have the Prime Minister's assurance that he will not breathe a word of Black's true identity to anyone. And let's face it — who'd believe him if he did?"

173

↯ The only way to defeat a Dementor is by casting the Patronus Charm; learn more on page 158

> "'Dumbledore's in charge, he founded it. It's the people who fought against You-Know-Who last time.'"
>
> HERMIONE GRANGER

ALBUS DUMBLEDORE
FOUNDER

MINERVA MCGONAGALL

RUBEUS HAGRID

CHARLIE WEASLEY

FRED WEASLEY

GEORGE WEASLEY

ARTHUR WEASLEY

MOLLY WEASLEY

Albus Dumbledore formed the original Order of the Phoenix to fight Lord Voldemort during the First Wizarding War.

NYMPHADORA TONKS

BILL WEASLEY

SEVERUS SNAPE

REMUS LUPIN

ALASTOR "MAD-EYE" MOODY

KINGSLEY SHACKLEBOLT

FLEUR DELACOUR

LILY POTTER

SIRIUS BLACK

Members of the Order have been taught by Dumbledore to communicate with each other using their Patronus. No witch or wizard can conjure another's Patronus, so there is no danger of false messages passing between members.

JAMES POTTER

HARRY POTTER

RON WEASLEY

HERMIONE GRANGER

PETER PETTIGREW

The Order of the Phoenix

BENJY FENWICK

HUNDUNGUS FLETCHER

ALICE LONGBOTTOM

The reformed Order has members old and new, but is composed only of overage wizards.

FABIAN PREWETT

ARABELLA FIGG

FRANK LONGBOTTOM

DORCAS MEADOWES

EMMELINE VANCE

Albus Dumbledore is the Secret Keeper for the Order; nobody can find its headquarters unless he tells them personally where it is.

GIDEON PREWETT

CARADOC DEARBORN

MARLENE MCKINNON

Dumbledore recalled the Order about an hour after the events of the Triwizard Tournament.

EDGAR BONES

ABERFORTH DUMBLEDORE

STURGIS PODMORE

DEDALUS DIGGLE

ELPHIAS DOGE

HESTIA JONES

Learn more about the Order's headquarters on page 80

7

BEASTS, BEINGS, AND BOTANICALS

The natural world that Muggles do not see is dangerous, spectacular, and endlessly surprising. A magical menagerie of wizarding pets, pests, dragons, and water creatures awaits. Learn about Herbology, the Care of Magical Creatures, and where in the world to find fantastic beasts in all their shapes and sizes. Those who are brave of heart might even wish to know what lurks in the mysterious shadows of the Forbidden Forest. . . .

WIZARDING PETS

Cats of every color

MAGICAL MENAGERIE   The shop in Diagon Alley sells all manner of pets. On a visit Harry sees . . .

> "'**F**eeling up to a
> long journey?'"

HEDWIG
~ OWNER ~
HARRY POTTER

> "'**A**ll the kids want
> owls, they're dead useful,
> carry yer mail an' everythin'.'"
>
> RUBEUS HAGRID

*A gift from
Hagrid, bought
at Eeylops Owl
Emporium*

*Harry found the
name "Hedwig" in
A History of Magic*

*The only snowy
owl at Hogwarts*

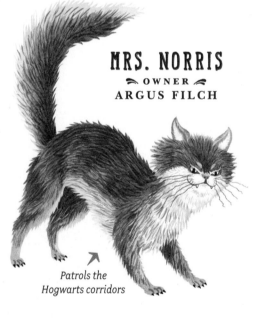

MRS. NORRIS
~ OWNER ~
ARGUS FILCH

*Patrols the
Hogwarts corridors*

*Hermione found him in the Magical
Menagerie in Diagon Alley*

*Enjoys chasing
spiders, rats,
gnomes, and
Snitches*

*Half cat, half
Kneazle, he is
highly intelligent
and able to identify
Animagi*

CROOKSHANKS
~ OWNER ~
**HERMIONE
GRANGER**

> "'**S**unshine, daisies, butter mellow,
> Turn this stupid, fat rat yellow.'"

SCABBERS
~ OWNER ~
**RON
WEASLEY**

*A hand-me-down
from Percy*

*Has never shown the
faintest trace of
interesting powers*

> "'**C**lever Crookshanks,
> did you catch that
> all by yourself?'"

⚡ Which pets are allowed at Hogwarts? Find out on page 19

A fat white rabbit that can change into a silk top hat

A Fire Crab with a jewel-encrusted shell

He can travel from place to place in a flash of flame

Like most phoenixes, Fawkes is gentle and very shy

A gift from Neville's great-uncle Algie for getting into Hogwarts

Neville keeps losing him, even on his first Hogwarts Express journey

TREVOR
OWNER
NEVILLE LONGBOTTOM

"'Oi, come back here, Trevor!'"

Will act to protect Dumbledore, and anyone who shows loyalty to him

Bred by Fred and George for Weasleys' Wizard Wheezes

FAWKES
COMPANION
ALBUS DUMBLEDORE

"'Fascinating creatures, phoenixes. They can carry immensely heavy loads, their tears have healing powers, and they make highly *faithful* pets.'"

ARNOLD
OWNER
GINNY WEASLEY

Ginny's Pygmy Puff

Sleek black rats

179

A gift from Sirius, small enough to fit in the palm of a hand

Ginny named him; Ron tried to change the name but it was too late

Likes to zoom around people's heads and hoot shrilly

PIGWIDGEON
OWNER
RON WEASLEY

"'Shut *up*, Pig.'"

A basket of funny custard-colored Puffskeins

ERROL
OWNER
THE WEASLEY FAMILY

Tends to collapse during deliveries

The Weasleys' ancient owl

HERMES
OWNER
PERCY WEASLEY

Percy's screech owl

Given as a gift for becoming a Prefect

HOUSEHOLD PESTS

There are many solutions to common wizarding pests (see *Gilderoy Lockhart's Guide to Household Pests*). However, in more extreme cases, it may be necessary to call in the Ministry of Magic's Department for the Regulation and Control of Magical Creatures (Pest Sub-Division).

Uses a high-pitched jabbering only understood by other pixies

Mostly found in Cornwall, England

"Fred, George, Harry, and Ron were the only ones who knew that the angel on top of the tree was actually a garden gnome that had bitten Fred on the ankle as he pulled up carrots for Christmas dinner."

Loves tricks and practical jokes

Expelled by swinging it in circles until dizzy and then dropping it over the garden wall

Common garden pest found throughout northern Europe and North America

PIXIE

The incantation "Peskipiksi Pesternomi" does not help at all when dealing with pixies

GNOME
FULL NAME IS
GERNUMBLI GARDENSI

Wingless but can fly; likes to seize unwary humans by the ears and deposit them at the tops of tall trees and buildings

"They grabbed ink bottles and sprayed the class with them, shredded books and papers, tore pictures from the walls, upended the wastebasket, grabbed bags and books and threw them out of the smashed window; within minutes, half the class was sheltering under desks and Neville was swinging from the iron chandelier in the ceiling."

Pursued by the Jarvey, a kind of overgrown ferret known for shouting rude words

See more gnomes outside the Burrow on page 82

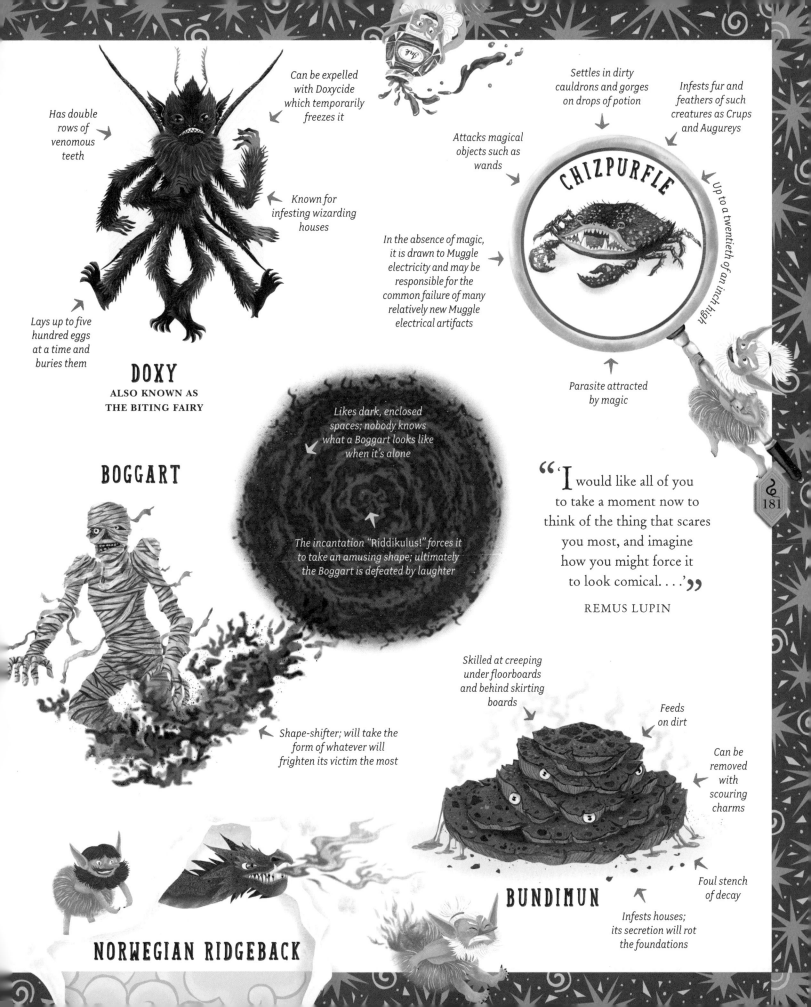

Has double rows of venomous teeth

Can be expelled with Doxycide which temporarily freezes it

Known for infesting wizarding houses

Lays up to five hundred eggs at a time and buries them

DOXY
ALSO KNOWN AS THE BITING FAIRY

Settles in dirty cauldrons and gorges on drops of potion

Infests fur and feathers of such creatures as Crups and Augureys

Attacks magical objects such as wands

CHIZPURFLE

Up to a twentieth of an inch high

In the absence of magic, it is drawn to Muggle electricity and may be responsible for the common failure of many relatively new Muggle electrical artifacts

Parasite attracted by magic

Likes dark, enclosed spaces; nobody knows what a Boggart looks like when it's alone

BOGGART

The incantation "Riddikulus!" forces it to take an amusing shape; ultimately the Boggart is defeated by laughter

"'I would like all of you to take a moment now to think of the thing that scares you most, and imagine how you might force it to look comical. . . .'"

REMUS LUPIN

181

Shape-shifter; will take the form of whatever will frighten its victim the most

Skilled at creeping under floorboards and behind skirting boards

Feeds on dirt

Can be removed with scouring charms

BUNDIMUN

Foul stench of decay

Infests houses; its secretion will rot the foundations

NORWEGIAN RIDGEBACK

More aggressive than its Welsh counterpart →

Requires a territory of up to a hundred square miles per dragon

↑ Grows up to thirty feet in length

HEBRIDEAN BLACK

Feeds on goats, sheep, and whenever possible, humans →

Has a fire-breathing range of up to fifty feet ↓

Will rarely kill unless hungry →

Dwells in valleys rather than mountains →

ANTIPODEAN OPALEYE

← Weighs between two and three tons

DRAGONS

"Probably the most famous of all magical beasts, dragons are among the most difficult to hide."

Named for its mushroom-shaped flame ↓

CHINESE FIREBALL

SWEDISH SHORT-SNOUT

Its flame can reduce timber and bone to ash in seconds →

Sometimes known as a Liondragon →

Weighs between two and four tons

Prefers wild, uninhabited mountainous areas

Aggressive but more tolerant of its own species than most dragons

HUNGARIAN HORNTAIL

Supposedly the most dangerous dragon breed

Uses its horns to gore prey before roasting it

Subject to an intensive breeding program to protect its numbers

ROMANIAN LONGHORN

Easily recognizable and melodious roar

COMMON WELSH GREEN

Smallest breed of dragon; approximately fifteen feet in length

Feeds on goats and cows, but has a strong liking for humans

PERUVIAN VIPERTOOTH

183

Nests in the higher Welsh mountains

Swiftest in flight

Extremely dangerous; crushes dwellings on which it lands

Slower in flight than some breeds

Attacks most large mammals, including water-dwelling creatures

Young breathe fire earlier than other breeds (between one and three months)

UKRAINIAN IRONBELLY

Largest breed of dragon; weighs up to six tons

NORWEGIAN RIDGEBACK

FIRE CRAB

Native to Fiji

Shoots flames from its rear end when attacked

"**M**erchieftainess Murcus has told us exactly what happened at the bottom of the lake, and we have therefore decided to award marks out of fifty for each of the champions, as follows. . . .'"

LUDO BAGMAN

MERPEOPLE

ALSO KNOWN AS SIRENS, SELKIES, MERROWS

Live worldwide in highly organized communities

Found on rocky coastlines of Europe

MACKLED MALACLAW

Aggressive to wizards and Muggles, domesticated by merpeople

Its bite will make the victim highly unlucky for up to a week

The oldest recorded merpeople were known as sirens (Greece)

Eats crustaceans and the feet of anyone foolish enough to step on it

MURTLAP

GRINDYLOW

WATER DEMON

Very long fingers with a powerful grip

Found in coastal Britain

GIANT SQUID

RAMORA

Powerfully magical; anchors ships and is a guardian of seafarers

Considered a pest by merpeople, who tie its rubbery legs in a knot; it drifts away and cannot return until it unties itself

Spines shred fishing nets

Found in the Indian Ocean

Nibbles the feet and clothing of swimmers

Found in the Atlantic Ocean

PLIMPY

Feeds at the bottom of lakes, ideally on water snails

SHRAKE

Created as revenge against Muggle fisherfolk who insulted a team of sailing wizards in the 1800s

WATER CREATURES

Found in Atlantic, Pacific, and Mediterranean seas →

SEA SERPENT

↑
Despite hysterical Muggle accounts, they are not known to have killed any humans

← Originated in Greece, usually found in the Mediterranean

HIPPOCAMPUS

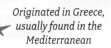

↑
Lays large, semi-transparent eggs in which the Tadfoal grows

LOBALUG

Merpeople use the Lobalug as a weapon →

Lives at the bottom of the North Sea ←

When threatened, it blasts the attacker with poison

Equally large in strength and stupidity

Prey ranges from wild animals to humans

Found in Scandinavia, Britain, Ireland, and northern Europe →

RIVER TROLL

Weighs over a ton →

If tricked into bowing, the water in the hollow of its head will run out, depriving it of all its strength

KAPPA
JAPANESE WATER DEMON

185

Feeds on human blood, but may not harm a person if it is thrown a cucumber with that person's name carved into it

The world's largest kelpie is found in Loch Ness, Scotland

Takes various shapes, often as a horse with bulrushes for a mane

Lures the unwary onto its back, then dives to the bottom of the river or lake →

KELPIE
BRITISH AND IRISH WATER DEMON

Can you find the famous kelpie on page 39?

Nifflers are attracted to anything that sparkles

DIGGING FOR TREASURE WITH NIFFLERS

CARE OF MAGICAL CREATURES

"**H**agrid was waiting for his class at the door of his hut. He stood in his moleskin overcoat, with Fang the boarhound at his heels, looking impatient to start."

To open The Monster Book of Monsters, *you have to stroke the spine*

HOW TO HANDLE A HIPPOGRIFF

Walk toward the Hippogriff. Make eye contact. Try not to blink.

Bow. Wait for the Hippogriff to bow in return.

You may now pat the Hippogriff.

To ride the Hippogriff, climb up behind the wing joint. Don't pull out any feathers.

Hold tight

FAVORITE FOODS

HIPPOGRIFFS: Insects, birds, and small mammals such as ferrets

BOWTRUCKLES: Woodlice, insects, or fairy eggs if they can get them

FLOBBERWORMS: Lettuce, but avoid overfeeding

SALAMANDERS: Flame; if fed pepper they can survive up to six hours outside a fire

THESTRALS: Raw meat; they're attracted to the smell of blood

ABRAXAN WINGED HORSES: Single-malt whisky

BLAST-ENDED SKREWTS: A mystery; try ant eggs, frog livers, grass-snake, dragon liver, or salamander eggs

THE BLAST-ENDED SKREWT PROJECT

OBJECTIVE: Raise Blast-Ended Skrewts from hatchlings to adults. Students must feed them, take them for walks, and try to make them hibernate.

CHALLENGES: The Skrewts keep attacking students and each other

SKREWT ORIGINS: Hagrid won't say

MAGICAL PROPERTIES: Unknown

DEFENSE MECHANISMS: Exploding rear ends, stings, suckers

SIZE: Hatchlings are six inches long, adults are ten feet

> "They're gettin' massive, mus' be nearly three foot long now. On'y trouble is, they've started killin' each other.'
>
> PROFESSOR HAGRID

SKREWT COUNT

SEPTEMBER: Start with hundreds of hatchlings
NOVEMBER: Twenty Skrewts left
DECEMBER: Down to ten
SPRING: Only two Skrewts remain . . .

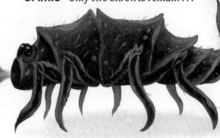

187

THE MINISTRY OF MAGIC DIVIDES ALL BEASTS, BEINGS, AND SPIRITS INTO FIVE CATEGORIES

or anything Hagrid likes

XXXXX Known wizard killer/impossible to train or domesticate

XXXX Dangerous/requires specialist knowledge/skilled wizard may handle

XXX Competent wizard should cope

XX Harmless/may be domesticated

X Boring

UNICORNS

> "They prefer the woman's touch, unicorns. Girls to the front, and approach with care, come on, easy does it. . . .'
>
> PROFESSOR GRUBBLY-PLANK

UNICORNS ARE HARD TO CATCH! YOU COULD TRY LOOKING IN THE FOREST . . .

UNICORNS have many magical properties in their horn, hair, and blood.

Foals are golden when born, turn silver after two years, and become white after seven.

FLUFFY
Gigantic three-headed dog

"'Yeah — he's mine — bought him off a Greek chappie I met in the pub las' year — I lent him to Dumbledore to guard the —' 'Yes?' said Harry eagerly. 'Now, don't ask me anymore,' said Hagrid gruffly. 'That's top secret, that is.'"

Fierce guardian →

"Slowly, the dog's growls ceased — it tottered on its paws and fell to its knees, then it slumped to the ground, fast asleep."

↑ *Easily falls asleep to music*

HAGRID'S PETS

Who wouldn't want pets that can burn, sting, and bite all at once?

← *Hatched from an egg by Hagrid, who won him in a card game with a mysterious stranger at the Hog's Head*

"When it bit me he told me off for frightening it. And when I left, he was singing it a lullaby.'"

RON WEASLEY

NORBERT
Norwegian Ridgeback dragon

"'Bless him, look, he knows his mummy!'"

RUBEUS HAGRID

Has his own teddy bear ↘

← *Fed with a bucket of brandy mixed with chicken blood every half an hour; grew three times in length in just one week*

↑ *Taken to Romania by Charlie Weasley's friends*

BUCKBEAK

Hippogriff

Also known as Witherwings

Enjoys a large plate of ferrets

> **"** 'Now, firs' thing yeh gotta know abou' hippogriffs is, they're proud,' said Hagrid. 'Easily offended, hippogriffs are. Don't never insult one, 'cause it might be the last thing yeh do.' **"**

Buckbeak was part of Hagrid's first lesson in Care of Magical Creatures

> **"** The hippogriff took off into the air. . . . He and his rider became smaller and smaller as Harry gazed after them . . . then a cloud drifted across the moon. . . . They were gone. **"**

Lots of slobber

Hatched from an egg by Hagrid, in a cupboard at Hogwarts

ARAGOG

Acromantula

Bit of a coward

> **"** 'A traveler gave me to Hagrid when I was an egg. Hagrid was only a boy, but he cared for me, hidden in a cupboard in the castle, feeding me on scraps from the table. Hagrid is my good friend, and a good man.' **"**
>
> ARAGOG

FANG

Enormous boarhound

Often found with Hagrid; very affectionate

Lives with his wife, Mosag, and their family in the Forbidden Forest

> **"** 'If anyone wanted ter find out some *stuff*, all they'd have ter do would be ter follow the *spiders*. That'd lead 'em right! That's all I'm sayin'.' **"**
>
> RUBEUS HAGRID

THE FORBIDDEN FOREST

1
CENTAURS
Firenze, Ronan, Bane, and
Magorian (left to right)

2
NIFFLER

3
BOWTRUCKLES

4
UNICORNS
Adult and foal

5
GIANT
Grawp

6
THESTRALS

7
ACROMANTULA
Aragog and Mosag

The Forest contains trees such as oak,
beech, and pine. Wanderers may also
find elder, holly, vine, and willow.

There are rumors that other creatures
have been seen in the Forest, including
werewolves, and even a Grim....

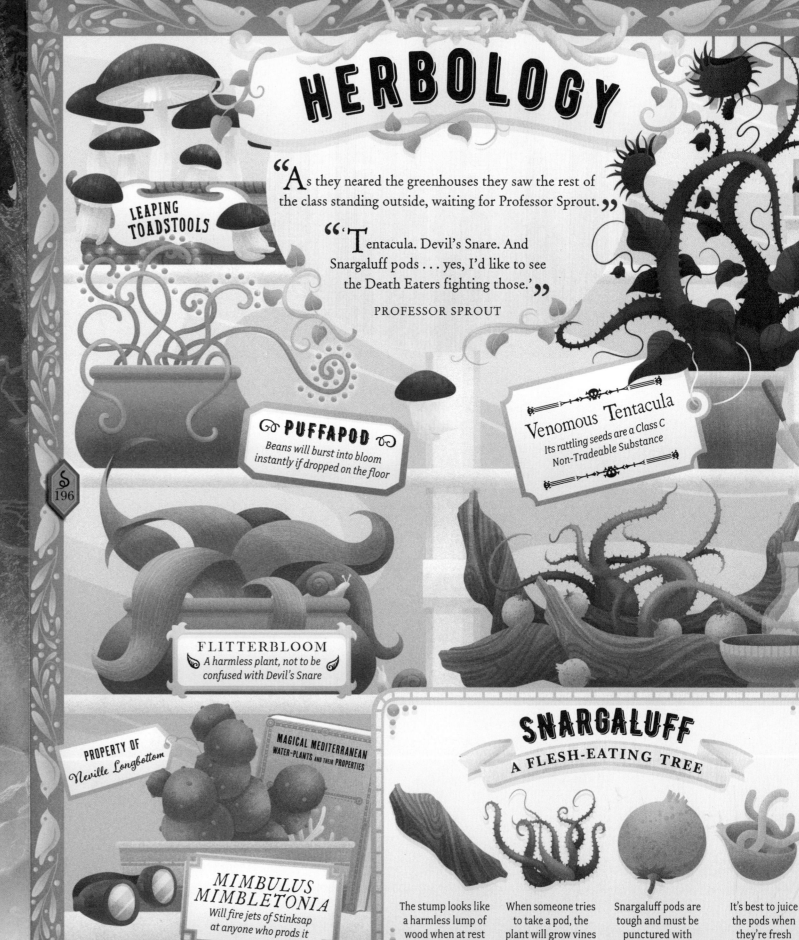

HERBOLOGY

LEAPING
TOADSTOOLS

"As they neared the greenhouses they saw the rest of
the class standing outside, waiting for Professor Sprout."

"'Tentacula. Devil's Snare. And
Snargaluff pods . . . yes, I'd like to see
the Death Eaters fighting those.'"

PROFESSOR SPROUT

PUFFAPOD
*Beans will burst into bloom
instantly if dropped on the floor*

Venomous Tentacula
*Its rattling seeds are a Class C
Non-Tradeable Substance*

196

FLITTERBLOOM
*A harmless plant, not to be
confused with Devil's Snare*

PROPERTY OF
Neville Longbottom

MAGICAL MEDITERRANEAN
WATER-PLANTS AND THEIR PROPERTIES

MIMBULUS
MIMBLETONIA
*Will fire jets of Stinksap
at anyone who prods it*

SNARGALUFF
A FLESH-EATING TREE

The stump looks like
a harmless lump of
wood when at rest

When someone tries
to take a pod, the
plant will grow vines
and attack them

Snargaluff pods are
tough and must be
punctured with
something sharp

It's best to juice
the pods when
they're fresh

See the water-plant Gillyweed on page 74

"Greenhouse Three housed far more interesting and dangerous plants."

MANDRAKE
(also known as *Mandragora*)
A powerful restorative used to return people who have been transfigured or cursed to their original state

Flutterby Bush
Can move and ripple its leaves

CAUTION

LIFE OF A
MANDRAKE

SIX MONTHS OLD
They become moody and secretive

SEEDLING
The cries of a young Mandrake can knock you out for several hours

MANDRAKE DRAUGHT
Mandrake forms an essential part of most antidotes

ADOLESCENT
BEWARE: likes to throw loud and raucous parties

CUT UP AND STEWED
Mandrake juice is collected

NINE MONTHS OLD
They start moving into each other's pots

MATURE
The cry of a fully grown Mandrake is fatal to anyone who hears it

CAUTION CAUTION

BUBOTUBER
Bubotuber pus is an excellent remedy for acne

WARNING
UNDILUTED PUS CAN CAUSE BOILS

DEVIL'S SNARE
Thrives in dark and damp environments; will seize anyone who comes too close

CAN CAUSE SUFFOCATION

197

ASIA

Kappa

Chinese Fireball

Winged Horse

Phoenix

Occamy

Demiguise

Ramora

"From darkest jungle to brightest desert, from mountain peak to marshy bog . . ."

FANTASTIC

WHERE TO

Hodag

Jobberknoll

Snallygaster

Wampus Cat

OCEANIA

Peruvian Vipertooth

Billywig

Fire Crab

Dugbog

THE AMERICAS

Shrake

Antipodean Opaleye

Sea Serpent

BRITISH ISLES

Leprechaun
Kelpie
Kneazle
Niffler
Common Welsh Green
Murtlap

EUROPE

Norwegian Ridgeback
Swedish Short-Snout
Hungarian Horntail
Troll
Hippogriff
Griffin

BEASTS AND FIND THEM

Centaur
Acromantula
FORBIDDEN FOREST
Thestral
Unicorn
Bowtruckle

Sphinx

AFRICA

Runespoor

HOGWARTS

Merpeople

HOGWARTS LAKE

Grindylow

Tebo
Fwooper
Erumpent
Diricawl

APPENDICES

THE CAST OF CHARACTERS
in a Completely Debatable Order of Appearance*

*PLEASE SEND YOUR COMPLAINTS TO DOLORES UMBRIDGE, CARE OF THE MINISTRY OF MAGIC

Harry Potter and the Sorcerer's Stone

VERNON DURSLEY • PETUNIA DURSLEY • DUDLEY DURSLEY
• PROFESSOR MINERVA MCGONAGALL • DEDALUS DIGGLE •
PROFESSOR ALBUS DUMBLEDORE • RUBEUS HAGRID • HARRY POTTER
• PIERS POLKISS • A BRAZILIAN BOA CONSTRICTOR • ARABELLA FIGG • TOM •
DORIS CROCKFORD • PROFESSOR QUIRINUS QUIRRELL • GRIPHOOK
• MADAM MALKIN • DRACO MALFOY • HEDWIG • GARRICK OLLIVANDER •
MOLLY WEASLEY • PERCY WEASLEY • FRED WEASLEY • GEORGE WEASLEY
• RON WEASLEY • HERMES • GINNY WEASLEY • NEVILLE LONGBOTTOM •
AUGUSTA LONGBOTTOM • LEE JORDAN • SCABBERS • THE TROLLEY WITCH
• HERMIONE GRANGER • VINCENT CRABBE • GREGORY GOYLE • TREVOR •
THE FAT FRIAR • NEARLY HEADLESS NICK (aka Sir Nicholas de Mimsy-Porpington)
• SEAMUS FINNIGAN • THE SORTING HAT • HANNAH ABBOTT • SUSAN BONES •
TERRY BOOT • MANDY BROCKLEHURST • LAVENDER BROWN • MILLICENT BULSTRODE
• JUSTIN FINCH-FLETCHLEY • MORAG MACDOUGAL • MOON • THEODORE NOTT •
PANSY PARKINSON • PADMA PATIL • PARVATI PATIL • SALLY-ANNE PERKS
• LISA TURPIN • BLAISE ZABINI • THE BLOODY BARON • PROFESSOR SEVERUS SNAPE •
PEEVES • THE FAT LADY • ARGUS FILCH • MRS. NORRIS • PROFESSOR POMONA SPROUT
• PROFESSOR CUTHBERT BINNS • PROFESSOR FILIUS FLITWICK • FANG •
MADAM ROLANDA HOOCH • OLIVER WOOD • DEAN THOMAS • FLUFFY
• ANGELINA JOHNSON • MARCUS FLINT • ALICIA SPINNET • KATIE BELL •
ADRIAN PUCEY • MILES BLETCHLEY • TERENCE HIGGS • MADAM IRMA PINCE
• LILY POTTER • JAMES POTTER • NORBERT • MADAM POPPY POMFREY • RONAN •
BANE • FIRENZE • THE GIANT SQUID • LORD VOLDEMORT

We first meet Minerva McGonagall not as a witch, but as a tabby cat, her Animagus form.

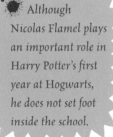

Although Nicolas Flamel plays an important role in Harry Potter's first year at Hogwarts, he does not set foot inside the school.

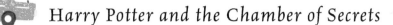

Harry Potter and the Chamber of Secrets

DOBBY • MR. MASON • MRS. MASON • ARTHUR WEASLEY • ERROL • LUCIUS MALFOY • MR. BORGIN • MR. GRANGER • MRS. GRANGER • PROFESSOR GILDEROY LOCKHART • COLIN CREEVEY • MOANING MYRTLE (*aka Myrtle Warren*) • THE WAILING WIDOW • SIR PATRICK DELANEY-PODMORE • ERNIE MACMILLAN • MISS FAWCETT • PROFESSOR AURORA SINISTRA • FAWKES • PENELOPE CLEARWATER • PROFESSOR ARMANDO DIPPET • TOM RIDDLE • ARAGOG • CORNELIUS FUDGE • THE BASILISK

Harry Potter and the Prisoner of Azkaban

MARJORIE DURSLEY • RIPPER • SIRIUS BLACK • STAN SHUNPIKE • ERNIE PRANG • MADAM MARSH • FLOREAN FORTESCUE • CROOKSHANKS • PROFESSOR REMUS LUPIN • SIR CADOGAN • PROFESSOR SYBILL TRELAWNEY • BUCKBEAK • CEDRIC DIGGORY • AMBROSIUS FLUME • MADAM ROSMERTA • DEREK • CHO CHANG • ROGER DAVIES • WARRINGTON • MONTAGUE • DERRICK • BOLE • WALDEN MACNAIR • PETER PETTIGREW • PIGWIDGEON

Sirius Black first appears to Harry when he mistakes him for the Grim, shortly before getting on the Knight Bus for the first time.

Buckbeak's would-be executioner, Walden Macnair, later reappears as a Death Eater.

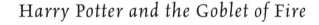

Harry Potter and the Goblet of Fire

MR. RIDDLE • MRS. RIDDLE • TOM RIDDLE SENIOR • DOT • FRANK BRYCE • NAGINI • BILL WEASLEY • CHARLIE WEASLEY • AMOS DIGGORY • BASIL • MR. ROBERTS • KEVIN • MRS. FINNIGAN • ARCHIE • CUTHBERT MOCKRIDGE • GILBERT WIMPLE • ARNOLD PEASEGOOD • BRODERICK BODE • CROAKER • LUDO BAGMAN • BARTY CROUCH SENIOR • WINKY • THE BULGARIAN MINISTER OF MAGIC • NARCISSA MALFOY • DIMITROV • IVANOVA • ZOGRAF • LEVSKI • VULCHANOV • VOLKOV • VIKTOR KRUM • CONNOLLY • BARRY RYAN • TROY • MULLET • MORAN • QUIGLEY • AIDAN LYNCH • HASSAN MOSTAFA • MRS. ROBERTS • DENNIS CREEVEY • STEWART ACKERLEY • MALCOLM BADDOCK • ELEANOR BRANSTONE • OWEN CAULDWELL • EMMA DOBBS • LAURA MADLEY • NATALIE MCDONALD • GRAHAM PRITCHARD • ORLA QUIRKE • KEVIN WHITBY • PROFESSOR ALASTOR "MAD-EYE" MOODY • MADAME OLYMPE MAXIME • PROFESSOR IGOR KARKAROFF • FLEUR DELACOUR • POLIAKOFF • VIOLET • RITA SKEETER • THE WEIRD SISTERS • STEBBINS • PROFESSOR WILHELMINA GRUBBLY-PLANK • GABRIELLE DELACOUR • MERCHIEFTAINESS MURCUS • MRS. CROUCH • BARTY CROUCH JUNIOR • BERTHA JORKINS • MRS. DIGGORY • APOLLINE DELACOUR • AVERY • MR. CRABBE • MR. GOYLE • MR. NOTT

Death Eaters are known for being shadowy, and their tendency to cover their faces with hoods and masks can make them difficult to identify.

There are several wizarding people who solely appear in photographs, although they remain important to Harry Potter's story.

Harry Potter and the Order of the Phoenix

MALCOLM • GORDON • MUNDUNGUS FLETCHER • NYMPHADORA TONKS • KINGSLEY SHACKLEBOLT • ELPHIAS DOGE • EMMELINE VANCE • STURGIS PODMORE • HESTIA JONES • MRS. BLACK • KREACHER • ERIC • BOB • PERKINS • AMELIA BONES • DOLORES UMBRIDGE • LUNA LOVEGOOD • EUAN ABERCROMBIE • ROSE ZELLER • ABERFORTH DUMBLEDORE • MARIETTA EDGECOMBE • ANTHONY GOLDSTEIN • MICHAEL CORNER • ZACHARIAS SMITH • PROFESSOR EVERARD • PROFESSOR DILYS DERWENT • PROFESSOR PHINEAS NIGELLUS BLACK • PROFESSOR DEXTER FORTESCUE • FRANK LONGBOTTOM • ALICE LONGBOTTOM • PROFESSOR SEPTIMA VECTOR • MADAM PUDDIFOOT • AUGUSTUS ROOKWOOD • DAWLISH • BRADLEY • GRAWP • MAGORIAN • PROFESSOR GRISELDA MARCHBANKS • DAPHNE GREENGRASS • PROFESSOR TOFTY • BELLATRIX LESTRANGE • ANTONIN DOLOHOV • WILLIAMSON

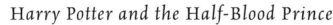

Harry Potter and the Half-Blood Prince

Caractacus Burke is one of the owners of the magical artifacts shop, Borgin and Burkes. He appears only in Dumbledore's Pensieve.

THE BRITISH PRIME MINISTER • ULICK GAMP • RUFUS SCRIMGEOUR • PROFESSOR HORACE SLUGHORN • VERITY • ARNOLD • ROMILDA VANE • CORMAC MCLAGGEN • MARCUS BELBY • JACK SLOPER • BOB OGDEN • MORFIN GAUNT • MARVOLO GAUNT • MEROPE GAUNT • CECILIA • DEMELZA ROBINS • JIMMY PEAKES • RITCHIE COOTE • LEANNE • CARACTACUS BURKE • MRS. COLE • URQUHART • HARPER • ELDRED WORPLE • SANGUINI • WILKIE TWYCROSS • CADWALLADER • HEPZIBAH SMITH • HOKEY • AMYCUS CARROW • ALECTO CARROW • FENRIR GRAYBACK

Harry Potter and the Deathly Hallows

Harry Potter's godson, Teddy Lupin, is only ever spoken about, not seen.

YAXLEY • PROFESSOR CHARITY BURBAGE • SELWYN • TED TONKS • ANDROMEDA TONKS • MONSIEUR DELACOUR • XENOPHILIUS LOVEGOOD • AUNTIE MURIEL • THORFINN ROWLE • MAFALDA HOPKIRK • REGINALD CATTERMOLE • ALBERT RUNCORN • PIUS THICKNESSE • WAKANDA • MARY CATTERMOLE • GREGOROVITCH • GELLERT GRINDELWALD • BATHILDA BAGSHOT • SCABIOR • TRAVERS • MARIUS • BOGROD • ARIANA DUMBLEDORE • THE GRAY LADY (aka Helena Ravenclaw) • LILY POTTER • ALBUS POTTER • JAMES POTTER • ROSE WEASLEY • HUGO WEASLEY • SCORPIUS MALFOY

Aberforth Dumbledore first appears in Harry Potter and the Order of the Phoenix in the Hog's Head, yet Harry doesn't realize who he is until Harry Potter and the Deathly Hallows.

MINISTERS OF MAGIC

1707–1718	Ulick Gamp *Founded the Department of Magical Law Enforcement*
1718–1726	Damocles Rowle
1726–1733	Perseus Parkinson
1733–1747	Eldritch Diggory *Established the Auror recruitment program*
1747–1752	Albert Boot
1752–1752	Basil Flack *Shortest-serving Minister*
1752–1770	Hesphaestus Gore
1770–1781	Maximilian Crowdy
1781–1789	Porteus Knatchbull
1789–1798	Unctuous Osbert
1798–1811	Artemisia Lufkin *Established the Department of International Magical Cooperation*
1811–1819	Grogan Stump *Established the Department of Magical Games and Sports*
1819–1827	Josephina Flint
1827–1835	Ottaline Gambol
1835–1841	Radolphus Lestrange *Attempted to close down the Department of Mysteries, which ignored him*
1841–1849	Hortensia Milliphutt
1849–1855	Evangeline Orpington
1855–1858	Priscilla Dupont
1858–1865	Dugald McPhail
1865–1903	Faris "Spout-hole" Spavin *Longest-serving Minister*
1903–1912	Venusia Crickerly
1912–1923	Archer Evermonde
1923–1925	Lorcan McLaird
1925–1939	Hector Fawley
1939–1948	Leonard Spencer-Moon
1948–1959	Wilhelmina Tuft
1959–1962	Ignatius Tuft
1962–1968	Nobby Leach
1968–1975	Eugenia Jenkins
1975–1980	Harold Minchum
1980–1990	Millicent Bagnold
1990–1996	Cornelius Fudge
1996–1997	Rufus Scrimgeour
1997–1998	Pius Thicknesse
1998–present	Kingsley Shacklebolt

The Full Lyrics to "WEASLEY IS OUR KING"

"*Weasley cannot save a thing,
He cannot block a single ring,
That's why Slytherins all sing:
Weasley is our King.*

*Weasley was born in a bin
He always lets the Quaffle in
Weasley will make sure we win
Weasley is our King.*

*Weasley is our King,
Weasley is our King,
He always lets the Quaffle in
Weasley is our King.*

*Weasley cannot save a thing,
He cannot block a single ring . . .*

*Weasley is our King,
Weasley is our King,
He didn't let the Quaffle in,
Weasley is our King . . .*

*Weasley can save anything,
He never leaves a single ring,
That's why Gryffindors all sing:
Weasley is our King.*

*Weasley is our King,
Weasley is our King,
He didn't let the Quaffle in,
Weasley is our King . . .*"

HARRY'S FIRST CHOCOLATE FROG CARDS

Albus Dumbledore,
Morgana, Hengist of Woodcroft,
Alberic Grunnion, Circe, Paracelsus,
Merlin, Cliodna

A COLLECTION OF COLORS

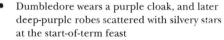

GREEN

- Harry has green eyes
- Harry remembers a green light from when Voldemort tried to kill him
- Slytherin colors are green and silver; their common room glows green from being located under the lake
- Letters from Hogwarts are addressed in green ink
- The writing that appears on the Marauder's Map is green
- Professor McGonagall wears an emerald cloak
- Dumbledore has green robes embroidered with many stars and moons
- Harry's dress robes are bottle green
- Mrs. Weasley gives Harry a hand-knitted emerald-green jumper
- Green smoke comes out of Harry's vault at Gringotts when it is opened
- Fireplaces burn emerald green with Floo powder
- Green wand sparks, high in the sky, signal that it's safe for Harry and the advance guard to leave Privet Drive on their broomsticks
- The drawing room of number twelve, Grimmauld Place has olive-green walls and moss-green velvet curtains
- The flash of light from the Killing Curse, Avada Kedavra, is green
- There is greenish glitter in the package containing the opal necklace that curses Katie Bell
- In the cave, the boat that carries Dumbledore and Harry across the black lake glows green, as does the chain that pulls it up out of the waters; the misty green glow at the center of the lake comes from a stone basin on an island, containing an emerald-green glowing liquid covering the locket

- Hagrid's motorcycle has a green button that makes a solid brick wall erupt from the exhaust pipe
- The Slytherin locket is as large as a chicken's egg, with an ornate letter "S" inlaid with small green stones
- Rita Skeeter's note to Bathilda Bagshot is written in spiky, acid-green writing
- Professor Slughorn wears emerald-green silk pajamas

PURPLE

- Dumbledore wears a purple cloak, and later deep-purple robes scattered with silvery stars at the start-of-term feast
- Professor Quirrell's turban is purple
- Cornelius Fudge wears purple boots
- The Knight Bus is purple
- Dumbledore conjures up purple sleeping bags for the Hogwarts students
- Letters from Hogwarts have a purple wax seal
- After eating the orange half of a Puking Pastille to get sick, swallowing the purple half restores you to full fitness
- An ancient set of purple robes tries to strangle Ron at Grimmauld Place
- Mrs. Weasley wears a quilted purple dressing gown
- Pale violet inter-departmental memos flit about the Ministry of Magic building
- The witches and wizards of the Wizengamot wear plum-colored robes with an elaborately worked "W" on the left-hand side of the chest
- The Ministry of Magic issues a purple leaflet about protection against Dark Forces
- As a Metamorphmagus, Tonks can change her appearance and sometimes makes her hair a violent shade of violet
- Harry and Neville's invitations from Professor Slughorn are parchment scrolls tied with violet ribbon
- Arthur Weasley's additions to Hagrid's flying motorbike include a purple button that blasts dragon fire out of the exhaust pipe
- The Weasleys' ghoul gets covered in purple blisters when it's enchanted to look as though it has spattergroit
- For Harry's seventeenth birthday meal, Hermione makes gold and purple streamers with her wand and drapes them over trees and bushes
- Mrs. Weasley wears a brand-new set of amethyst-colored robes with a matching hat to Bill and Fleur's wedding
- Hermione wears a floaty, lilac-colored dress with matching high heels
- There's a purple carpet in the wedding marquee
- There are purple carpets in the corridors of Level One at the Ministry of Magic
- Xenophilius Lovegood's tea, made from Gurdyroots, is as deeply purple as beetroot juice
- The walls of the Malfoys' drawing room are dark purple
- Luna tells Dean about creatures with tiny ears a bit like a hippo's, only purple and hairy, that she says will come if you hum to them — preferably a waltz, nothing too fast

A PRICE LIST FROM THE WIZARDING WORLD

Glittery black beetle eyes from the apothecary	5 Knuts a scoop
Floo powder	2 Sickles a scoop
Society for the Promotion of Elfish Welfare (S.P.E.W.) membership and badge	2 Sickles
Three Butterbeers from the Hog's Head	6 Sickles
A bag of Knarl quills from Mundungus Fletcher	6 Sickles
Weasleys' Wizard Wheezes Canary Cream	7 Sickles each
A trip on the Knight Bus from Magnolia Crescent to London	11 Sickles
A trip on the Knight Bus from number twelve, Grimmauld Place to Hogwarts	11 Sickles
Some of everything from the trolley on the Hogwarts Express	11 Sickles and 7 Knuts
A trip on the Knight Bus from Magnolia Crescent to London, with hot chocolate	13 Sickles
A trip on the Knight Bus with a hot-water bottle and a toothbrush in the color of your choice	15 Sickles
A black-and-gold quill from Scrivenshaft's Quill Shop	15 Sickles and 2 Knuts
Dragon liver from the apothecary	16 Sickles an ounce
Two coffees at Madam Puddifoot's	1 Galleon
Weasleys' Wizard Wheezes Headless Hats	2 Galleons each
Basic Blaze box of Weasleys' Wildfire Whiz-bangs	5 Galleons
Harry's wand from Ollivanders	7 Galleons
A copy of *Advanced Potion-Making* from Flourish and Blotts	9 Galleons
Venomous Tentacula seeds from Mundungus Fletcher (bought by Fred and George Weasley for their Skiving Snackboxes)	10 Galleons
Omnioculars at the Quidditch World Cup	10 Galleons
Metamorph-Medals	10 Galleons
Salazar Slytherin's locket (bought by Caractacus Burke from Merope Gaunt)	10 Galleons
A twelve-week course of Apparition Lessons from a Ministry of Magic Apparition Instructor	12 Galleons
A pint of Baruffio's Brain Elixir (sold by Eddie Carmichael)	12 Galleons
A skull from Borgin and Burkes	16 Galleons
Silver unicorn horns	21 Galleons each
A pint of Acromantula venom (a rough estimate according to Horace Slughorn)	100 Galleons
A cursed necklace from Borgin and Burkes	1,500 Galleons
The price on Sirius Black's head	10,000 Galleons
A lot of information	"generated by a fat bag of Galleons"
The price on Harry Potter's head	10,000 Galleons
Harry Potter and his wand (according to Fenrir Grayback)	200,000 Galleons
The sword of Godric Gryffindor	"a small fortune"

WANTED
HARRY POTTER

REWARD
G10,000

K·B

FLOO POWDER

S.P.E.W.

CANARY CREAM

HEADLESS HATS
WWW

OWL POST

Special Deliveries

FIRST YEAR

- Hagrid pulls a ruffled owl from his pocket and writes to Dumbledore to say he's found Harry

- An owl delivers the *Daily Prophet* to Hagrid on the Hut-on-the-Rock and attacks his coat looking for payment

- Hedwig makes her debut delivery on Harry's first Friday at Hogwarts, with an invitation to tea at Hagrid's hut

- Draco Malfoy's eagle owl regularly brings him sweets and cakes from home

- A barn owl drops off Neville's Remembrall from his grandmother

- Six large screech owls carry in Harry's Nimbus Two Thousand, a secret gift from McGonagall

- Hagrid sends owls to James and Lily's school friends asking them to post back pictures, to make a photo album for Harry

SECOND YEAR

- A barn owl delivers an underage sorcery warning to Harry in the Privet Drive dining room, dropping the letter on Mrs. Mason's head

- Errol collapses in the Weasleys' armchair after taking Hermione's letter to the Burrow

- Neville's grandmother often sends things he's forgotten at the start of term

- Errol falls into a milk jug on the Gryffindor table after bringing Ron a Howler from Molly

THIRD YEAR

- Errol, unconscious, is carried by two other owls into Harry's bedroom while delivering a Sneakoscope from Ron

- A huge barn owl delivers a Howler to Neville from his grandmother

- Pigwidgeon flies into Ron's life carrying a letter from Sirius to Harry on the Hogwarts Express

FOURTH YEAR

- Sirius sends Harry letters at Privet Drive using brightly colored birds

- Harry sends Hedwig from Privet Drive to ask his friends for food; Hermione sends her back with sugar-free snacks

- Errol needs five days to recover after bringing Harry an enormous fruitcake and assorted pasties from the Burrow

- On Harry's fourteenth birthday, four owls bring four birthday cakes, one each from Ron, Hermione, Hagrid, and Sirius

- Pigwidgeon delivers Harry's invitation to the Quidditch World Cup final

- People keep posting Howlers to the Ministry, reducing Percy's best quill to cinders

- Pigwidgeon and two school screech owls carry an entire ham to Sirius in Hogsmeade

- One morning a gray owl, four barn owls, a brown owl, and a tawny owl deliver hate mail to Hermione, including an envelope full of Bubotuber pus

- Fred and George use a school barn owl to send blackmail to Ludo Bagman

- Before the third task of the Triwizard Tournament, Sirius sends Harry a good-luck card: a folded piece of parchment decorated with a muddy paw print

FIFTH YEAR

- Five owls swoop or crash into Privet Drive in one evening, carrying messages for Harry about the Ministry of Magic's hearing

- Hermione borrows Hedwig to tell her parents about becoming a Prefect

- Hermes brings a message to Ron from Percy, warning Ron that the Ministry is at odds with Harry

- Numerous owls land at the Gryffindor table bringing Harry letters of support, as well as a screech owl bearing a copy of his *Quibbler* interview

SIXTH YEAR

- The Ministry sends leaflets by owl, containing not-very-useful security advice against the Death Eaters

- Three handsome tawnies arrive with Harry, Ron, and Hermione's O.W.L. results

SEVENTH YEAR

- During the height of the Second Wizarding War, Fred and George continue to operate their Owl Order business out of Auntie Muriel's back room

· J.K. ROWLING ·

J.K. ROWLING is the author of the enduringly popular, era-defining Harry Potter seven-book series, which has sold over 600 million copies in 85 languages, been listened to as audiobooks for over one billion hours, and made into eight smash hit movies. To accompany the series, she wrote three short companion volumes for charity, including *Fantastic Beasts and Where to Find Them*, which went on to inspire a new series of films featuring Magizoologist Newt Scamander. Harry's story as a grown-up was continued in a stage play, *Harry Potter and the Cursed Child*, which J.K. Rowling wrote with playwright Jack Thorne and director John Tiffany.

In 2020, she returned to publishing for younger children with the fairy tale *The Ickabog*, the royalties for which she donated to her charitable trust, Volant, to help charities working to alleviate the social effects of the COVID-19 pandemic. Her latest children's novel, *The Christmas Pig*, was published in 2021.

J.K. Rowling has received many awards and honors for her writing, including for her detective series written under the name Robert Galbraith. She supports a wide number of humanitarian causes through Volant, and is the founder of the international children's care reform charity Lumos. J.K. Rowling lives in Scotland with her family.

To find out more about J.K. Rowling, visit jkrowlingstories.com.

· ACKNOWLEDGMENTS ·

· CONTRIBUTORS ·
Dave Brown — Ape Inc Ltd., Amanda Carroll, Tom Hartley, Ceri Woods

Stephanie Amster, Mandy Archer, Clare Baggaley, Jessica Bellman,
Jacqui Butler, Jessica George, Sarah Goodwin, Claire Henry,
Rosie Mearns, Gemma Sharpe, Abby Shaw, Jadene Squires,
Danielle Webster-Jones from Bloomsbury

Ross Fraser and Chloë Wallace from The Blair Partnership

· ARTIST CREDITS ·

· PETER GOES ·
Pages 70–71, 72–73, 86–87, 90–95, 96–97, 118–119,
124–125, 130–131, 146–147, 168–169, 170–171, 172–173

· LOUISE LOCKHART ·
Pages 40–41, 48–49, 52–53, 54–55, 56–57, 200–201, 202–203, 204–205, 206

· WEITONG MAI ·
Pages 16–17, 22–23, 24–25, 26–27, 28–29, 30–31, 32–33, 74–75, 76–77,
116–117, 136–137, 138–139, 144–145, 150–151, 166–167, 196–197

· OLIA MUZA ·
Pages 18–19, 68–69, 78–79, 112–113, 114–115, 188–189

· PHAM QUANG PHUC ·
Pages 34–35, 44–45, 60–61, 62–63, 66–67, 120–121, 134–135,
142–143, 148–149, 162–163, 178–179, 180–181, 182–183, 184–185,
186–187, 198–199 and the cover illustration

· LEVI PINFOLD ·
Pages 50–51, 98–99, 100–101, 102–103, 104–105,
126–127, 128–129, 156–157, 158–159, 174–175, 190–195

· TOMISLAV TOMIĆ ·
Pages 10–11, 12–13, 20–21, 38–39, 42–43, 46–47,
58–59, 80–81, 82–83, 84–85, 106–107, 108–109, 110–111,
122–123, 140–141, 152–153, 154–155, 164–165